CITY OF
LIFESTONE

STORIES IN AN AGE OF FANTASY

STORIES FROM THE FAR FUTURE

WARPED GALAXIES

WARHAMMER
ADVENTURES
STORIES IN AN AGE OF FANTASY

REALM QUEST

CITY OF

LIFESTONE

TOM HUDDLESTON

WARHAMMER ADVENTURES

First published in Great Britain in 2019 by
Warhammer Publishing,
Willow Road,
Nottingham, NG7 2WS, UK.

10 9 8 7 6 5 4 3 2 1

Produced by Games Workshop in Nottingham.
Cover illustration by Cole Marchetti.
Internal illustrations by Magnus Norén & Cole Marchetti.

A CIP record for this book is available from the British Library.

ISBN 13: 978 1 78496 782 6

See Warhammer Adventures on the internet at

warhammeradventures.com

Find out more about Games Workshop and the worlds of
Warhammer 40,000 and Warhammer Age of Sigmar at

games-workshop.com

Printed and bound by CPI Group (UK) Ltd, Croydon, CR0 4YY

For my cohort Cavan Scott, with immense gratitude.

Contents

The Mortal Realms

Each of the Mortal Realms is a world unto itself, steeped in powerful magic. Seemingly infinite in size, there are endless possibilities for discovery and adventure: floating cities and enchanted woodlands, noble beings and dread beasts beyond imagination. But in every corner of the realms, battles rage between the armies of Order and the forces of Chaos. This centuries-long war must be won if the realms are to live in peace and freedom.

One year ago...

The great beast soared on tattered
wings, riding a current of stifling air.
Its cry echoed from the stony slopes
as it spotted another fearful runaway,
sprinting for the shelter of a ravine.
The creature lowered its black beak,
long tail lashing with an audible thrum.
Then it folded its hooked pinions and
dived. Kiri heard a startled shout, then
silence.

'Get moving!'

The scar-faced barbarian raised his
whip and Kiri stumbled forwards, the
black boulder balanced between her
shoulder blades. Ahead of her a line

of shuffling, bent-backed figures went winding up the mountainside, dusty brown rags clinging to their scrawny, sweating bodies. The sun was a dull copper coin wreathed in black cloud, and the air was sulphur-scented and sweltering. Here in Aqshy it was always hot. They didn't call it the Realm of Fire for nothing.

Huge fortifications loomed over her, half-built ramparts and shield walls topped with leering stone beast-heads and twisted mystic symbols that hurt Kiri's eyes just to look at. The walls clung to the mountain's peak, a vast black fortress constructed to protect... what? No one in the slave camp was entirely sure. Some said it was an ancient artefact, a mystical weapon that could turn the tide of this centuries-long war. Others claimed that the mountain was the resting place of some dormant creature, a fire-drake of impossible size that the Darkoath Barbarians planned to unleash against their enemies. But the wisest suspected that behind those ramparts was a Realmgate – a doorway between the worlds, and a strategic gift to whichever side managed to claim it. This last idea appealed most to Kiri. The thought that just behind that hulking pile of hewn rock might lie a way out of this nightmare... well, that was just too good to be true. Meaning, of course, that it probably wasn't.

The last push up the scree-slope was always the worst, the ground shifting and sliding and threatening to topple her. But Kiri managed to scramble to the top, unloading her burden onto a pile of misshapen stones in the shadow of the outer wall. Straightening, she allowed herself a moment to appreciate the sudden weightlessness in her limbs before it was time to go back for another load. Her eyes stung, her body was riddled with scrapes and bruises and her limbs were ready to collapse. But – for those few seconds – she felt almost human.

On the slopes below the slave camp she could make out the Darkoath horde, wedged defensively between the arms of the mountain. From up here they looked like a nest of vermin, clad in boiled leather and dull armour, black-furred warhounds straining at the leash. When the citadel was completed they would occupy it, but until then they were exposed, out here in the open. That's why they keep telling us to work faster, Kiri thought. They're afraid of what might be coming.

A hand touched her sleeve and Kiri jerked round, ready to tell the master how sorry she was for slacking. But she found herself looking into the windswept face of a young man, his red-rimmed eyes filled with sympathy. Kiri knew right away what that meant.

'Kellan,' she said. 'It's time?'

Kellan nodded quickly. 'Go. I'll distract him.'

He took a step towards the scarred

slavemaster, falling to his knees and begging for water. The barbarian sneered, kicking Kellan down with one booted foot. Kiri took her chance and bolted, scurrying back down the slope and through a shallow ravine, emerging into the maze of canvas structures and smouldering ash-heaps that had been her home these past months. Or had it been longer? She could barely recall her life before the Darkoaths took them.

She reached the tent, preparing to duck inside. Then for a moment she thought she saw a shadow on the horizon, shifting and rising. Coming closer? It was hard to tell; the Cindercaust Mountains were coloured entirely in shades of black and grey. But this was a different kind of darkness, a fog covering the far peaks one by one as it rolled in. For a moment she thought she felt a cool breeze on her face.

Then her mother called out and Kiri pushed into the tent. Chetan lay

wrapped in a thin sheet on a patch of
smooth ground that Kiri had cleared for
her. Her eyes twitched open and she
smiled through cracked lips. Kiri knelt,
and Chetan struggled up to embrace
her. Her skin was like dry paper, the
bones of her hands almost weightless.
But Kiri could still feel the pulse of life
inside.

Chetan pulled her daughter close. 'It's
time… to leave,' she whispered, holding
Kiri's gaze.

Kiri feigned surprise. 'But mum, I only just got here.'

Chetan laughed despite herself, but it soon turned to coughing. 'No jokes,' she said. Then her hand squeezed a little tighter, her voice growing stronger. 'We talked about this, Kiri. We've looked after each other this long, but there's nothing you can do for me now. I won't let you die a slave. Find a way out, take any risk you have to take, but *go home.*'

'To Lifestone,' Kiri said. She'd heard so many stories of her birth city that she almost felt she knew the place. Chetan had been born there, had spent her youth among its gardens and orchards. She'd fallen in love, been married, and twelve years ago she'd given birth to a daughter. Then some cataclysm had forced them to leave, to wander the wilds, to fall into the hands of slavers. Kiri wasn't sure why her mother had abandoned the city she loved so much. Chetan didn't seem to know herself, it had just... happened.

'Lifestone,' Chetan said, savouring the word. She turned Kiri's arm over, exposing the black birthmark on the inside of her wrist, a smooth circle with an arrow projecting from it. 'Find the city. Make a better life. Promise me.'

Kiri nodded. 'I'll try.'

Chetan shook her head. 'Don't try.' Her words were little more than a hoarse gasp. 'Promise.'

Kiri turned away as the tears came. 'I promise.'

Chetan slumped, her chest rising and falling, rising and falling, each time a little slower. Kiri hung her head. It was the way of things, she knew that. And wherever her mother was going, it had to be better than this. But still, her heart ached. Finally, Chetan's hand slipped from her grasp, and she lay still.

'Lazy little wretch,' a voice snarled and a hand reached into the tent, dragging Kiri out. The barbarian leered, swollen lips drawing back over foul yellow teeth. 'I'll teach you to go slinking off for a nap.'

Kiri twisted away and his whip glanced off her shoulder. 'No,' she protested. 'My mother... She's...'

'She's what?' the slaver asked. 'Dead? She won't be the only one if you don't get moving.'

He reached out with a leathery fist, pulling Kiri towards him. She felt the grief and horror rising up inside, threatening to overwhelm her. *No.* There'd be time for that later. She smelled the slaver's putrid stench, tasted ash in her mouth and heard her mother's voice one last time.

Promise me.

Kiri twisted, swinging her fist as hard as she could.

Her blow caught the slaver on the jaw and he cried out in surprise, losing his balance and landing hard on his backside. Kiri's home-made catapult was strapped to her waist, beneath her rags. She snapped it loose, slipping in a lump of shot from the secret pouch sewn into her cloak. But before she could take aim, everything changed.

Lightning struck the slopes below, jagged forks of electricity slicing down through the still air. She recalled that shadow on the horizon; somehow it had overtaken them, a churning storm front circling overhead. The lightning bolts descended from it, and where they struck Kiri saw a flash of gold, like a beacon in the darkness.

Horns blared and drums boomed as the Darkoath horde sprang into action. Swords and axes were hastily drawn, and she heard a mighty roar and groan as a hideous troll-like troggoth was unleashed from its cage, lumbering into the fray. Lightning struck again, and again, and she heard the clash of swords.

The scar-faced barbarian picked himself up, rubbing his jaw. Two of his fellows came lumbering in, gripping steel clubs. Kiri raised her catapult, watching keenly as they circled closer.

Then a voice rang out in the valley, louder than any voice she'd ever heard or imagined. It was deep and resonant, shaking the very stones beneath her feet. Far down the slope a figure stood alone, gleaming gold in the darkness.

'In the name of Sigmar,' it proclaimed, and she saw the barbarians clutching their ears and staggering as though the sound itself was excruciating. 'Prepare to be destroyed.'

The slavers fell to their knees, wailing. Kiri drew herself up, the voice from the valley filling her with a kind of wild hope. She gritted her teeth and ran.

She headed back uphill, realising she had no idea where she was going. All around she could see her fellow slaves gazing in awe down the mountainside, their work forgotten.

Kellan ran towards her. His eyes were shining. 'The Army of Sigmar,' he said.

'They've come to save us!'

But Kiri wasn't sure it was that simple. Yes, Sigmar's soldiers fought to restore order – her mother had told her all about the mighty king in his celestial realm of Azyr. His forces might break the barbarian lines; they might batter down these unfinished fortifications and claim whatever was inside. But the battle would be fierce, and anyone caught in the middle could expect no mercy.

'We can't stay here,' she told Kellan. 'My mother's gone, she's... We have to run, while there's still time.'

But Kellan shook his head, crouching to pick up a large rock. 'No, Kiri,' he said. 'We have to fight.' He raised his fist defiantly, and looking around Kiri saw others doing the same.

'For Sigmar!' they shouted. 'For Azyr!'

Kellan charged up the hillside, other slaves rallying to his call. Above them loomed the half-built keep, those hideous stone faces shifting in every flash of lightning. Kiri started after him, then stopped herself. *Wait,* she thought, *I should be running away.* But somehow, her feet didn't want to.

Hearing shouts, she saw the three slavers moving to cut her off, their boots gripping the scree. She ducked under the wooden scaffold at the base of the wall, where a heap of loose boulders lay waiting to be lifted into position. Crouching, she tugged out the wooden pikes that held the rock pile in place, giving the uppermost boulder a hard shove. The rocks rolled free and tumbled down the slope, the barbarians scrambling desperately out of the way.

Then she heard a crash, and a loud creak. One of the rocks had slammed into the base of the scaffold, jarring it. Slaves peered over the edge. The scaffold groaned as another boulder struck it.

'Jump!' Kiri shouted, crouching in the shelter of a huge flat stone as the scaffold began to fall. She saw men leaping to safety as the entire structure collapsed, the outer wall slumping as its support weakened. The stone beast-heads toppled, snarling mouths biting sand as they hit the ground and rolled, the great fortification sliding in pieces down the mountainside.

A cheer went up, and as the dust cleared Kiri saw men and women grabbing stones and wooden stakes. More slavers charged in but their captives fought back, overwhelming the barbarians through sheer force of numbers. Whips cracked and fists flew, and any sense of order disintegrated.

Kiri scrambled over the wreckage of the outer wall, moving deeper into the half-built stronghold. She had no idea where she was going. Or did she? It was as though a voice were calling to her; she couldn't hear it but she knew what it was saying. She'd never felt anything so strange.

She dropped into what would've been the courtyard, an open space between the outer wall and the keep itself. An archway opened ahead of her, a black mouth leading deeper into the fortress. Around the entrance foul signs and symbols had been carved, seeming to shift and writhe beneath her gaze. She shuddered. But that was where the voice, or the feeling, was telling her to go.

Shouts erupted as groups of slaves came bounding over the wall, running to join their fellows inside the courtyard. She saw Kellan among them, handing out pikes and swords taken from fallen slavers. Then the ground began to shake, a deep drumming emerging from the tunnel. One by one they turned to the archway.

The barbarians charged into the courtyard three abreast, their faces leering in the dusty light. Their swords were notched, their armour clattering with skulls and sigils. Their warhounds sprang forwards, attacking without mercy, driving the slaves back. Kiri saw blood on the stones. The battle would be a short one.

She looked up at the dark doorway. The way was blocked with tumbling bodies, but the urge to enter was somehow stronger than her fear. She started forwards.

The first barbarian who came at her went down easily – one catapult shot between the eyes and he dropped, shouting. The next took her by surprise, but she spun and pushed him into a group of armed slaves, who swiftly overwhelmed him. The archway was close now. She was going to make it.

Then five more figures emerged from the darkness and her heart sank. Kiri raised her catapult but there were too many, their whips and blades lashing closer. She dodged back and their lunges missed; she ducked and their whips snapped overhead. But she was surrounded on all sides – there was no way out.

There was a roar of thunder. The

ground shook. Her attackers froze, staring up into the sky.

The eye of the storm was directly overhead, the darkness whirling as the wind raged. Stones rattled from the high walls of the keep, slamming into the courtyard. The very air felt charged.

Lightning struck the courtyard, a bolt of pure white shattering the flagstones. Kiri rubbed her eyes, the flash imprinted on her lids. When she looked again a figure stood there, face masked, golden armour rippling in the light. It

was a man; his sword was drawn, his blue cloak whipping in the wind.

Kiri gasped. A Stormcast Eternal. She'd heard tales of their bravery all her life, but never expected to come face-to-face with one. Sigmar's fiercest warriors rode the lightning into the heart of battle, wherever their strength was needed most. Their helms were spiked with a golden crown and their shields bore the symbol of Ghal Maraz, the fabled hammer of King Sigmar himself. Kiri grinned. These barbarians wouldn't stand a chance.

Lightning struck again, and again. Two more figures appeared in the courtyard, then two more, and two more. Slaves and masters alike stared in wonder as Sigmar's warriors took their battle stance, marching in lockstep across the bloody courtyard. The barbarians roared and charged. Kiri couldn't tear her eyes away.

Then she felt a sudden pain and grabbed her wrist. Her birthmark was on fire, as though her skin had been branded. And in that moment she knew: this was the source of the voice inside her. The mark had been guiding her, leading her on, and it couldn't stand to wait.

She fled through the archway into a broad, unlit tunnel, trying not to look at the twisted inhuman figures hewn into the walls on either side. The cries of slavers rang in her ears as she ran, entering a large round room of bare rock, the roof open to the sky. Ahead of her was a perfect circle of polished stone, around ten times her height. Looking into that dark frame she could see nothing but the far wall; it was just an empty ring, with pale runes carved upon it. Could this be what all these people had been trying, and dying, to protect?

She took a step closer. There, near the base of the circle, was a rune she recognised. It was the same symbol she bore, her birthmark tingling as she approached. Energy crackled and inside the circle of black stone she could make out a faint red glow, a threaded web sewn into the empty air. She'd never seen a Realmgate before; at least, not that she could remember. But somehow she knew this was one. A portal into another world, awake and calling to her.

For a moment, she paused. What would await her when she stepped through? The gate could lead anywhere – to the Realm of Shadows, or Light, or Death or... yes, it might lead to Ghyran, the Realm of Life, where the city of Lifestone waited to welcome her home.

The stones of the citadel echoed with the din of battle. Lightning arced overhead, again and again, as more Stormcast Eternals joined the fray. Soon they would claim their prize; the Realmgate would be theirs, and she'd never know what lay on the other side. Balling her fists, she stepped closer.

Wisps of red energy darted towards her, and she felt the hairs on her skin stand upright.

Kiri took a breath. What was she waiting for?

She stepped into the circle, and vanished.

CHAPTER ONE

The Silent Market

The direwolf's jaws snapped and Kiri
threw herself sideways, tumbling into
a rocky ravine. Thorny bushes snagged
at her cloak as she picked herself up,
loading her catapult. The wolf bounded
alongside, its shaggy black mane
outlined against the tall trees and the
pale sky. Up ahead she could see her
travelling companion, Harvin, casting
a panicked look back as he fled, his
pedlar's pack clanking with copper pots
and iron tools.

Then the wolf darted closer, paws
scrabbling on the edge of the ravine,
preparing to spring. Kiri loosed her

shot, and to her satisfaction it struck the creature square on the snout. The direwolf whined, sprawling in the dirt. Kiri put on a burst of speed, hearing the creature scrabble to its feet and continue the pursuit.

They'd been running since dawn. A fallen bridge had delayed them the day before, forcing them to camp in the forest. Kiri had been woken by strange sounds and a smell of decay, the air so cold she could see her breath. Then the direwolf had attacked, bounding from the darkness, threatening to drag Harvin away until a shot from Kiri's catapult drove it back. They hadn't had a moment to rest since.

But in truth, Kiri reflected, she'd been running for the better part of a year. Yes, the Realmgate had brought her to Ghyran, just as she'd hoped. But that had been her last stroke of luck – from then on, every day had been fight or flight. The Realm of Life was rightly named, every corner of it overrun with living things. The trouble was, most of them wanted to eat her. She'd battled packs of gryph-hounds in the Nevergreen Mountains and had spent two nights trapped in the nest of a long-tailed cockatrice, a meal for its caterwauling fledglings. And the towns weren't much better: the street gangs in the great city of Hammerhal were as dangerous as any wolfpack.

She glanced back, expecting the direwolf to be hard behind them. But to her surprise the animal had fallen back, sitting on its haunches and narrowing its yellow eyes. Kiri slowed her pace, tugging on Harvin's sleeve.

'What's it doing?' she hissed. 'Waiting for reinforcements?'

The pedlar shook his head. 'I told you we'd be safe if we made it to Lifestone – those hairy fiends won't go near the place. And here we are. Look.'

He pointed and Kiri raised her eyes, tugging back her grey headscarf. A wide valley fell ahead, the trees replaced by slopes of scrub-grass and stony soil. Beyond was a wall of dark mountains, rising peak upon jagged peak to the limits of her vision. But closer, at the valley's head, was a sprawling shadow, a darkness that couldn't be natural.

A city. Lifestone.

Kiri's heart tightened. This couldn't be the place her mother had sent her to find – the city was wreathed in mist and shadow, a flock of noisy ravens circling overhead. Rain began

to fall, a thin drizzle that somehow made her feel even more sweaty and uncomfortable.

'Are you sure this is right?' she asked. 'I mean, absolutely sure?'

Harvin smiled, displaying his last remaining teeth. She'd met him on the road six days before, and he'd offered his guidance. He was a decent sort – a little slow-witted, perhaps, but generous with his supplies.

'I've been peddling up and down this road all my born days. You think I don't know where I'm going?'

'But Lifestone is a place of healing,' Kiri insisted, recalling her mother's words. 'There are gardens, and orchards and sparkling fountains. There's... life!'

Harvin shrugged. 'Once upon a time, maybe. When I was young they said this was the place to go if you had wounds that wouldn't heal, and not just on the outside if you know what I mean. You had to walk a hard road to find it, but it was worth the effort.'

'So what happened?' Kiri asked.

Harvin shrugged, hitching up his trousers. 'I dunno. The crops went bad, I s'pose. People moved away. This is how it's been for as long as I remember. Sorry it's not what you was expecting.'

Kiri tightened her fists until her knuckles turned white. Somewhere deep down she'd known it would be this way, that the city Chetan spoke of was just a figment of her imagination. Years of servitude had twisted her mother's mind – who could blame her for retreating into some half-dreamed vision of the past?

That didn't make it any easier, though. Because buried beneath all those doubts and fears, Kiri had also carried a little flame of hope. Hope that her mother's words would prove true, hope that she would find Lifestone and all her hardships would be over.

That flame had just flickered out.

They drew closer, and now she could

make out individual buildings – wooden shacks nestled together in the crook of the valley, with larger, more ornate structures of hewn grey stone on the higher slopes. But even these once mighty manses looked battered and worn down – she saw fallen arches and crumbling spires, their jagged tops like dogs' teeth biting at the sky. At the top of the rise was a structure paler than the rest, a huge white palace of towers and parapets, all centred around a coloured glass dome that sparkled in the light. But even this was falling into disrepair, its walls shrouded with vines, its minarets crumbling.

Ruined buildings were commonplace in Ghyran, of course; centuries of war had left even mighty Hammerhal in pieces. But this was different somehow – she didn't see any scorch marks or cannon-holes, no signs of battle or siege. The place seemed to have simply fallen apart, and no one had bothered to repair it.

Kiri gritted her teeth, fighting down a wave of despair. She was strong, she told herself, stronger than she'd ever been. Life in the slave camp had toughened her body, while a year in the wilderness had done the same for her mind. The reason for this disappointment was because she'd let herself hope in the first place. But that hope was gone now; it couldn't hurt her any more. She would become as hard and unbending as life itself.

The outer wall of Lifestone rose above them, ravens crowing from the battlements. This at least seemed intact, a sturdy fortification of granite boulders so huge it must've taken a team of rhinox to haul them. The road led through an arch beneath a raised portcullis, and the two of them followed.

Harvin nodded to the Freeguild soldier minding the gate, a scruffy slob in a tatty black uniform with the faded symbol of a fountain stitched on the breast. He didn't respond, picking his teeth with the point of his dagger. They passed into a massive courtyard, and Kiri stopped dead in surprise. The space was packed with stalls and busy with people, but all she heard was silence.

She'd been to markets all across the realm – they were good places to pick up work and news and, if she was desperate, to steal a bite to eat. But from the vast covered pavilions of Hammerhal to the tiniest village fayre they each had one thing in common – noise. Traders' cries, furious haggling, angry curses and joyful greetings, these were the lifeblood of any Ghyran bazaar.

Except, apparently, this one. Figures moved from stall to stall, selecting goods and handing over their coins; she saw men and women, children and old folk, their faces stern and joyless as they heaped their baskets with grain and root vegetables, hard bread and eggs the size of Kiri's head. A sign above a herbalist's stall read 'Put the Spring Back in your Step with Archimband's Amazing Unguent!', but the words were faded and the owner looked as miserable as everyone else.

Hinges creaked ominously and Kiri saw a sign outside an old tavern: 'The Fountain', it read, clearly a popular symbol in these parts. She peered through the inn's filthy windows and saw men at the bar, perched on high stools in total silence. A rough-looking gang of stout, short-legged Duardin sat in the shadows of an alcove, smoking long pipes and staring sullenly into their stone tankards. She wondered if there were any Aelf-folk in Lifestone, but it seemed unlikely – the Wanderers were surely too proud to show their faces in a dump like this.

Harvin led her across the courtyard to a stall selling cookware, where a burly young man peered at them from below a dull green awning. 'Expected you yesterday,' he grunted as Harvin began to unpack, lining his wares up on the counter.

'We hit trouble on the road,' he said. 'Had to spend the night in the Stonewoods.'

The stallholder frowned, his bushy eyebrows meeting in the middle. 'You don't want to do that. There's been stories.'

'What sort of stories?' Kiri asked.

He scowled down at her. 'Who are you meant to be?'

'That's Kiri,' Harvin said. 'I showed her the way here.'

'Why would anyone want to come here?' the stallholder sneered. 'Anyhow, Lord Elias sent a party of his best Freeguild soldiers into the Stonewoods last month, hunting Tuskers for his table. They never came back.'

Harvin's eyes widened. 'I thought I heard something in the trees last night. Didn't you, Kiri?'

'There's been other tales too,' the young man went on, gesturing up the hill. 'Giant rats up near the old theatre, walking on their hind legs and wearing clothes. Skaven, they say.'

'Skaven?' Harvin snorted. 'They're just a kids' story.'

The young man shrugged. 'Just telling you what I heard.'

'What happened here?' Kiri asked, unable to hold her tongue any longer. 'Where are the orchards and the gardens? Where are the houses of healing? And why is everything so *quiet*?'

'I don't know what you're on about,' the young man snapped. 'This is Lifestone – this is how it's always been. Now go away, I'm not buying.' He thrust Harvin's goods off his counter and dropped the awning.

The pedlar turned to Kiri apologetically. 'Brodwin's never been friendly, but that's rude even for him.'

She looked around. 'I thought Ghyran was the Lady Alarielle's realm, the Realm of Life. But this place is about as lively as a mortuary. You said it used to be different, so what changed?'

Harvin shook his head, then he pointed up between the narrow buildings. 'There's a Sigmarite temple about three streets thataway. They always used to have a bed and broth for a weary traveller, and they might have some answers for you, too.'

Kiri nodded. 'Thank you. For everything. You're the first person in a long time who's actually been kind to me.' Harvin smiled and she grinned back. Then she remembered what she'd decided about being hard and unbending and straightened her face.

She weaved through the shuffling market crowds, the silence weighing her down. She saw a butcher carving up a rhinox carcass, hacking at it glumly with a blunt cleaver. A horse surprised her and she jumped, backing into a man hauling three baskets of wheat. He glared, gathering up his load and moving on. *It's all wrong*, she thought.

*He should've yelled at me and made
a scene.* She'd have been happier if he
had.

The rough buildings rose above her as
she headed for the street Harvin had
gestured to. The rain was falling harder
now, drumming on the canvas stalls
and wooden roofs.

Then a soft voice said, 'Girl,' and Kiri
turned. A lady in black stood beneath
the awning of an apothecary's shop,
crystal flasks and copper alembics
gleaming in the window. Her face
was half-hidden beneath a fur-lined
hood and her elegant black robe was
finely stitched with silken thread. She
beckoned and Kiri joined her beneath
the awning.

'Share my shelter, child.' The lady
smiled through pale lips. Then she
gestured subtly towards the courtyard.
'I wonder, did you know you're being
watched?'

Kiri looked up in time to see a man
in the crowd turning away, his head

wreathed in smoke from a curved arkenwood pipe. He was tall and thin, with greying hair almost to his shoulders. He wore a black hat with a wide brim and carried a wooden staff.

'He's been following you,' the hooded lady said. 'Around here folks call him the Shadowcaster, though Child Snatcher would be a better name, if you ask me. He takes children, they say, and carries them off to that big palace on the hill.'

Kiri felt her pulse quicken. The man didn't glance back, stalking away through the market, his staff tapping on the cobbles. He was soon lost in the crowd.

'Perhaps you should go,' the hooded lady whispered. 'Now, while he's not looking.'

'Thank you,' Kiri said gratefully. Then she ducked into the rainswept streets and ran.

CHAPTER TWO

The Mark

The temple was right where Harvin
had said it would be, a once proud
edifice of sandy stone topped with a
crumbling bell tower. The bell itself was
huge, its hammer moulded to resemble
Ghal Maraz, the weapon of Sigmar.
But both bell and hammer were dark
with rust, and the statue of the Lady
Alarielle that stood on the steps below
was patched with lichen. When Kiri
banged on the heavy wooden door she
could hear nothing inside but echoes.

She sank down at the statue's feet,
pulling her scarf up over her head.
There was nothing for her in this

dead city, she was sure of it now. Her mother must have meant well, but the Lifestone of Chetan's youth was gone. So where in all the realms was Kiri supposed to go now? This had been her only goal, her only purpose. Without it she was just another aimless, homeless orphan, like a thousand thousand others.

'You need guidance,' a voice said, and Kiri sprang to her feet. She was expecting a Sigmarite priest in his patterned plate and chainmail, but instead found herself facing a tall, grey-haired man – the Shadowcaster, she realised; the one from the market. The one the hooded lady had warned her about.

He puffed his pipe and frowned, and Kiri took a step back.

'N-no. I'm fine.'

'Are you sure?' His deep blue eyes seemed to sparkle beneath the circumference of his hat. 'You seem... lost.'

'I'm not,' Kiri said, backing away. There was something in that sharp stare that made her nervous, as though he knew something about her that even she didn't know. 'My dad's waiting. And my, um, six big brothers.'

'You're here alone,' the Shadowcaster said, stepping towards her. 'I know why you came.'

'You don't know anything about me,' Kiri spat. 'Just leave me alone!'

And she broke into a run, darting away across the square. As she reached the far side she glanced back, sure that he would be right behind her. But he was still standing in the shadow of the temple, watching her curiously.

She hurried away, through a narrow downward-sloping street lined with hunched wooden houses and shops with faded signs and dusty windows. The roofs seemed to lean together, looming like an arch of dark trees. But the way was straight, and Kiri knew exactly where she was going – she'd follow this street back down to the market, then maybe she'd search out that lady apothecary and ask her advice.

Then abruptly the street ended and she stopped, surprised. She was in a little courtyard, a dry fountain in the centre topped with another statue of Alarielle, her body wreathed in stone flowers. One arm was raised, but the hand had snapped off leaving a rough stump. In the corner of the square a group of children in home-made masks were playing at being Stormcasts, waving their wooden swords in total silence.

Kiri shook her head, confused. Had she turned without realising it? Or had she taken the wrong street to begin with? The city seemed bigger than it had appeared from outside, revealing more of itself with every twist and turn.

She crossed the courtyard, choosing another road that led downhill. Surely it would lead to the market eventually, or at least to the city wall. She took a turning, then another. Now she was moving uphill. She didn't want that. She backed up, retracing her steps. An uncertain feeling was building inside her. She clutched her wrist, pressing her fingers against her birthmark. She could feel it tingling, adding to her sense of unease.

She broke into a run, taking turns at random, breaking from shadow into light and back again. She was moving so fast that she didn't see the boy until she was right on top of him. He looked up in surprise as she slammed into him and they crashed to the floor, landing in a tangle of limbs.

Kiri shoved the boy away. 'Get off me!'

'B-but you ran into me,' he protested, sitting up. He was short, wiry and black-haired, dressed in a loose grey robe with dull steel bracers and shin-guards. His skin was so pale it was almost translucent, and his grey eyes were sunk into the hollows of his sharp, watchful face.

Kiri leapt to her feet, suddenly annoyed. 'You should've looked where you were going, shouldn't you? Is everyone in this city half-asleep, or are you all just really stupid?'

The boy's mouth dropped open. 'I... I don't...'

'Do you know how far I travelled to get here?' Kiri went on, her frustration spilling out. 'I nearly died, more times than I can count. I fought gangs of bandits, and packs of direwolves. And for what?'

The boy climbed to his feet and Kiri braced, reaching for her catapult. To her surprise, it wasn't there. The boy backed away, one hand inside his robes.

'Thief,' Kiri snarled. 'You're a thief!' She strode towards him, holding out her hand. 'Give it. Now.'

The boy sighed and handed her catapult back sheepishly. Then he gasped in disbelief. 'Your arm!'

Kiri flushed, covering her wrist. 'What about it? You never saw a birthmark before?'

'Yes,' the boy said. 'I have.'

He turned his hand over and there on his white skin was a black mark. It wasn't identical to Kiri's – the symbol was different, a line with a spike jutting from it rather than the circle-and-arrow printed on her own flesh. But they were the same shade of ebony, and located in precisely the same place.

'You're one of us,' he said, reaching for her. 'You have to come with me.'

'You have to back off, thief,' Kiri said, slapping his hand away.

The boy turned abruptly, cupping his hands and calling out. 'Thanis! Alish! Come quick!'

Kiri looked around. The street seemed deserted. Then a figure strode around the corner, moving fast. It was a girl, taller than Kiri and broader too, with flame-red hair and skin the colour of dry sand. She looked like a fighter, with powerful muscles and a breastplate emblazoned with the twin-tailed comet of Sigmar. On her hands were gloves of interlocking steel, creaking as she flexed her fingers.

'Kaspar?' she asked, lumbering closer. 'What's up? You found them rats?'

She was carrying something on her back – a pack, or a weapon, or... No, Kiri realised, it was a person, hopping down onto the cobbles and hurrying towards them. This was a girl too, short and spry with bunches in her hair. Tools clattered in a belt at her waist and there was a hammer strapped to her back with a steel head half the size of Kiri's own. She looked a little young to be an engineer or an inventor, but anything was possible.

'She's got the mark,' the boy was saying, gesturing to Kiri's wrist.

The smaller girl's eyes widened. 'Hammer of Grungni, he's right. Thanis, don't let her run.'

The tough-looking one circled Kiri. 'You got to come with us,' she said. Then she turned her wrist and Kiri saw another mark imprinted there, shaped like a key with a hook curving from it. 'My name's Thanis. This is Alish, and Kaspar you already met. We're your friends, honest.'

'Some friends,' Kiri snarled. 'That boy stole my catapult.'

Alish nodded ruefully. 'He does that. I bet he's sorry.'

'Not as sorry as he's going to be,' Kiri growled.

'Now listen,' Thanis said, her cheeks flushed. 'Before I lose my temper. You think you're tough, but you're out of your depth here. So just come with us, and there'll be no need to— Kaspar, grab her!'

The boy had circled behind Kiri and now he lunged in, trying to take hold. But she kicked back, lightning quick, sending him flying across the cobbles. Kiri backed up, loading her catapult and aiming it at Thanis.

'Nice try,' she said. 'Do that again and it'll hurt.'

'It already hurts,' groaned the boy.

Thanis seethed, her cheeks flushing. 'We're not messing around,' she said. 'You come along, now, before I do something I'll feel bad about.'

Kiri stared, sizing her up. Then she shook her head. 'I don't think so,' she said, and bolted.

She fled uphill this time, ducking through a vine-wreathed arch into a wide road lined with bare trees, their branches like bones in the dim light. She could hear the others calling after her and put her head down, breaking left, back down the slope. She took another turn, and another, sure by now that she'd put plenty of space between herself and those strange children. How was it even possible they all bore the same kind of birthmark?

She slowed, approaching another square – not the market, but she had to be close. She stepped into the sunlight and her mouth fell open. Just ahead of her were three familiar figures – one tall, one short and one skinny. The boy spotted her first and pointed, the big girl sprinting towards Kiri, a snarl on her face.

'Get back here!'

Kiri backed away, her head spinning. It wasn't possible – she'd come so far; how could they have tracked her? She darted right and right again, hurtling down long streets. The houses closed in around her and she felt panic rising in her gut. The city seemed determined to trick and confuse her – every time she thought she knew where she was she'd look up and see that the sun wasn't where it had been, or that the slope of the hill had twisted at right angles to where it was last time.

She turned into another broad

thoroughfare and almost screamed. There they were again, rounding a corner just a short distance away. Her head spun as she staggered into a narrow alleyway, sweat coursing down her back. She could hear their shouts, their feet ringing on the stones. She took one last turning and gave a cry of rage as she found herself facing a wall of cracked red bricks. She booted the wall in frustration. The voices drew closer.

Then she felt shifting shadows on her face and looked up. A tree grew over the wall, a single knotted branch with a few dead leaves clinging to it. It wasn't much, but it was a chance. She stepped back, giving herself a run-up. Then she sprinted and leapt, using the wall for leverage. She grasped the branch, hearing it groan as she swung up and over the wall.

She dropped silently on the other side. She could hear muffled voices beyond the wall, full of confusion and disappointment. She smiled and started forwards, pushing through a dense thicket of trees.

She stopped, startled. A figure stood there, grey and hooded, perched atop a stone plinth in the centre of an overgrown garden. It was a statue, she realised, but a very lifelike one – she kept her eyes fixed on it as she drew closer, half expecting it to turn towards her. It clasped a long-bladed scythe in bony hands, and beneath the hood was a gaunt face, almost skeletal in appearance.

Kiri shivered. The statue was unnervingly realistic, its eyes sunk so deep that they seemed almost bottomless. Symbols were scratched on the plinth below, twisted death-runes and baleful marks cut into the stone. She tore her gaze away, those blank eyes watching her as she moved towards a tall building that loomed imposingly over her.

This, too, made Kiri's skin crawl. It

was narrow, pale and high-sided, with rows of black windows rising up towards the low clouds – she tried to count the levels and somehow couldn't get a grasp on the number, as though her eyes and mind kept slipping. She peered through the ground floor window and saw scorch marks on the walls, as if a fire had swept through this building and gutted it from the inside out.

It seemed deserted, she reflected; it might be a good place to hide out until she was sure those kids had gone. But as soon as the idea came to her, she rejected it – the thought of actually entering this grim, haunted structure was too much to bear.

So she turned away, glancing back at the statue, making sure it hadn't crept up on her. It stood where it always had, scythe raised as the rain fell. A narrow passageway ran along the edge of the building and she hurried through it, emerging into another drab, deserted street.

But as she stepped out she heard those voices again, distant but drawing closer. Would they never give up? Across the street was a curved brick building, crumbling and clearly abandoned. The windows were boarded, but as she approached Kiri saw that one of them had been forced open, the planks pried loose. She peered in. There was no bad feeling here, just a strong smell of dust and damp. So she climbed inside, dropping over the sill. The dust on the floor was marked with footprints – splayed feet with three toes. Some kind of animal? If so, it walked on two legs – her time in the mountains had taught her to know the difference.

A sign hung on the wall, and she wiped the dust from it with her sleeve. The words 'Upper Circle' were painted in age-worn lettering, an arrow pointing to a flight of steps that led up into the dark. She climbed, and before she reached the top she could hear voices.

CHAPTER THREE

Ratmen

The top stair creaked, and Kiri
froze. But the voices kept speaking,
somewhere in the darkness up ahead.
She emerged into an impressive, almost
circular hall. The ceiling was adorned
with flaking frescoes depicting scenes
from the Age of Myth – she saw
Alarielle planting soulpods in a wooded
glade, and Sigmar riding into battle
on the back of his mighty Stardrake.
Daylight slanted through rotted holes
in the roof, illuminating rows of wooden
benches. She moved between them,
coming to a low barrier and peering
cautiously over the edge. Beneath the

balcony was a wooden stage, and on the stage was the oddest creature she had ever seen.

It had two furred legs and two clawed arms, throwing them wide as it spoke. It wore a purple waistcoat and a sable cloak, and its red eyes glimmered above a twitching, fang-filled snout. Kiri had always assumed the Skaven were a myth, a bedtime story to frighten misbehaving children. But this walking, talking ratman was very real indeed.

'My lady calls and quick-quick comes Kreech. Her wish is my command, yes-yes!' The Skaven sniggered, as though sharing a secret. 'Oh fine-fine lady, oh good-best queen, Kreech is yours to use as you desire, yes-yes! Or so it seems. Am I right, my dutiful Lesh?'

Kiri crouched, peeping over the railing. There was another figure in the shadows, a large, black-furred Skaven with dirty white robes stretched over a tight round belly.

'True-true, most high Packlord Kreech,' he snickered. 'You are her trusted agent, her good-good captain. Great riches await, surely-surely.'

The first Skaven smiled, hideous lips drawing back over pointed teeth. 'Riches, yes-yes. But more than that, oh Lesh. Infamy. Respect. Fear! They take us for fools-fools, but we'll show them. Yes-yes, we will.'

Kiri ducked, backing away. There was no telling how many more of these monsters might be lurking around. But as she started to turn a hand grabbed her shoulder, another clamping over her mouth.

'Quiet,' a voice hissed. 'If those things hear us we're in proper trouble.'

The hands pulled away and Kiri twisted, her back to the railing. The tough girl, Thanis, was crouching in front of her, one finger pressed to her lips. Behind her Kiri could see the others, little Alish with her hammer and that thieving boy, Kaspar, hunched in the shadows with his hooded cloak wrapped around him.

'How did you find me?' she whispered.

Thanis held out her wrist. 'The marks. When there's three of us we can sort of tell where someone is.'

'Vertigan calls it Triumverance,' Alish added. 'But I was the one who figured it out.'

Kiri shook her head. 'I thought the streets were moving.'

'Maybe they were,' Kaspar said.

'Sometimes I think this city's got a mind of its own.'

'That's just your excuse for always getting lost.' Alish grinned. 'Look, we found the rats like Vertigan wanted. Can we go home now?'

'Only if she'll come with us,' Thanis said, nodding at Kiri.

Kiri sighed. 'Where is this... home?'

'It's called the Arbour,' Alish said. 'We live there, with Elio and our master, Vertigan. He brought us together.'

Kiri's eyes narrowed, then she nodded. 'All right. Lead the way.' She'd play along for now, and once they were clear of these ratmen she'd look for another way to escape.

Kaspar crept back towards the stairway, the others at his back. With a start, Kiri realised that the voice from below them had ceased. She peered over the balcony. There was no sign of the Skaven.

'Wait,' she hissed. But it was too late.

Kaspar stepped back out of the stairwell, his eyes wide. Over his shoulder Kiri could see a dark figure, and another, and another. The ratmen swarmed silently up the steps, their claws raised. They were shorter than the one on the stage, scantily armoured in boiled leather. But there were so many of them, and more pouring in all the time. Kiri could see cold light in their red eyes.

Alish cried out, and the Skaven answered with a screech of pure animal savagery. They charged up the steps, claws scraping on the narrow walls. They were almost upon them.

'Help me with this,' Thanis barked at Kiri, her muscles straining as she lifted one of the long wooden benches. 'Grab that end. Now turn it.'

Together they angled the bench so that it was aiming down the steps. Thanis gave a shove, driving it down like a ram. The ratmen tumbled into one another, landing in a heap.

The black-robed Skaven put his head into the stairway, letting out a chittering cry of anger and disgust. 'Fools-fools!' he cried. 'Don't just lie there! Get them!'

The creatures gathered themselves and started up, scrambling over the fallen bench.

'They're coming again,' Alish said, unclipping the hammer from her back and swinging it in front of her. 'We need to get out of here.'

'Look!' Kaspar said, pulling his hood back and pointing up into the rafters. Above the stage was a metal gantry with ropes hanging from it. 'Thanis, boost me up. It might be a way out.'

The tall girl cupped her hands and Kaspar stepped into them, steadying himself on the top of her head.

'Three, two...' Thanis gave a mighty shove and he sprang into the air, fingers scrabbling on the rusty gantry. Kiri's breath stopped as Kaspar hung one-handed above the stage. Then he swung and grabbed on, pulling himself up.

'Nothing to it,' he said, his face flushed.

'For you, maybe,' Thanis said. 'But how are the rest of us meant to get up there?'

'We don't go up, we go down,' Alish said. 'Kaspar, toss one of those ropes to Thanis.'

Kaspar nodded, grabbing a rope and tying it fast to the gantry before throwing the loose end down. Thanis caught it, wrapping it around her wrist. 'Will it hold?'

Kaspar bounced on the metal platform. It creaked but seemed sturdy. 'Hopefully.'

Thanis held out a hand to Alish, and the smaller girl turned. But one of the Skaven leapt from the stairwell behind her, slashing with a blunt blade. Alish stumbled in surprise, dropping her hammer.

'Sigmar's beard!' she spluttered as the creature's sword swiped overhead, missing her by a hair. The Skaven raised it again, letting out a gleeful cackle.

Kiri's catapult shot took the creature under the chin, and its laughter turned to a gurgle of surprise. Kiri grabbed Alish, pulling her to her feet and returning her hammer. Alish clipped it onto her back, then she took hold of Thanis's arm.

'You too,' Thanis told Kiri, her hand outstretched.

Kiri looked up uncertainly. 'Are you sure that rope'll hold us all?'

'No choice!' Thanis cried, tugging her forward. Kiri felt wind on the back of her neck as a sword sliced the air. She clutched Thanis's waist and they toppled over the edge of the balcony, swinging out into empty space.

They hurtled towards the stage and over it, the rope groaning, Alish's whoop of excitement ringing in Kiri's ears. The rope was strong, but as they swung back she heard a creak and a snap, and looked up to see the gantry above them crumpling, and finally breaking in two.

They hit the stage with a thump, tangled in the heavy curtains. Thanis struggled to her feet, swaying dizzily. Then there was a cry overhead and she looked up, holding out her arms as something dropped right into them.

'Thanks,' Kaspar said, grinning up at Thanis. 'I guess it wasn't as secure as I thought.'

With a clang, the gantry landed in

two pieces on the stage.

'You're lucky,' Thanis said. 'You always got me around to catch you.'

Hearing a screech, Kiri looked up. The Skaven crowded along the upper railing, waving their swords and making rude gestures. Some were climbing over and dropping from the balcony, while others bounded through an opening at the back of the auditorium, swarming towards the stage.

'We should leave,' she said. 'Right now.'

Thanis led them to the back of the stage, where a stout wooden door was held shut with a loop of rusty chain. She charged, striking the door with all her strength. The chain snapped and it sprang open.

Kiri looked back to see the Skaven coming after them, blinking in the daylight. The black-robed leader pushed forward, gesticulating wildly.

'What are you stop-waiting for?' he screeched. 'After them!'

CHAPTER FOUR

Vertigan

Kiri spun, loosing her catapult, hearing a satisfying screech. Kaspar sprinted at her side, swift and silent. Thanis followed with Alish balanced on her shoulders, the tools in her belt rattling noisily. Behind them came a writhing mass of Skaven, a wild stampede of claws and teeth and ragged brown fur.

The creatures were clutching swords and whips and all manner of blunt implements. Their leader brought up the rear, waving his skinny arms and crying in a shrill voice: 'Quick-quick! Get them!'

The street was deserted but Kiri

saw faces peering from high windows, mouths dropping open as the tide of ratmen swept through the city. She almost smiled. That ought to wake them up a bit.

'This way,' Kaspar said, pulling her into an alleyway between high wooden fences. The little thief seemed to know where he was going, but so had she right before she got completely lost. Then the alley opened out and she felt a wave of relief.

Heads turned as they hurtled into the market square. 'Run!' Alish yelled from her high perch. 'The Skaven are coming!' But people just stared, their expressions ranging from mild irritation to complete disbelief.

The din built behind them and Kiri wheeled to see the ratmen emerging into the square, claws and weapons drawn. The inhabitants of Lifestone turned, slack-jawed, unable to believe their eyes. Then at last they started to move, shoving and scrambling in panic.

Stalls collapsed and carts were toppled as they ran for cover, and somewhere nearby a bell began to ring.

The Skaven spread out, frenzied with excitement – Kiri saw one of them snatching a bucket from a woman's hands and burying its snout inside. It came up grinning, its furry jaws dripping with milk. Another two leapt on a rich trader, tearing the gold chain from his neck.

'No-no, leave them!' the leader

bellowed, gesticulating furiously. 'We're not here to plunder and chew-chew! Grab the child-things!'

Kiri whirled round, realising she'd lost the others in the confusion. Then she saw Kaspar a short distance away, coming to a halt within a ring of market stalls. Thanis was with him, whipping round as two Skaven came bounding over the back of a leaning coal-cart, moving to cut them off. Alish dropped from her back, unclipping her hammer and swinging it by the handle. The ratmen closed in.

Kiri took cover, watching breathlessly. The two Skaven were joined by several more, their claws outstretched as they bore down on the three children. Thanis grabbed two of them in her gloved hands, knocking their furry heads together. Alish swung her hammer and knocked the backboard off the coal-cart, burying three startled ratmen in a pile of black nuggets. Kaspar stayed low, grabbing lumps of coal and hurling them. But more Skaven were already swarming towards them.

Kiri bit her lip. She could run in and help, maybe take down a Skaven or two, but what good would it do? These creatures were out for blood. *Remember what you told yourself*, she thought. *You are alone. You are tough. All you can do is look after yourself.*

Then a voice called out, 'Girl-thing. Do not move.'

The Skaven leader strode through the melee, his cloak billowing. He gave a smile that was more like a grimace, holding up his leathery, clawed hands.

'Stay away from me,' Kiri hissed, raising her catapult. 'I'll shoot you, I swear.'

'No-no,' Kreech said again, tilting his head. 'You don't see, girl-thing. We have you caught.'

The large Skaven appeared behind Kiri, grabbing her by both arms, squeezing her wrists so hard that her catapult clattered to the ground. She struggled but the creature was too strong.

'Hold her, good-good Lesh,' Kreech grinned. 'Don't let her flee-flee.'

Kiri heard a high-pitched cry, and craning her neck she saw that Alish had been captured too, kicking madly at the two Skaven holding her. Kaspar struggled as they swarmed over him, and even Thanis was driven down, bellowing furiously as they forced her to the cobbles.

Then there was a flash of light and a voice spoke, so loud that Kiri's head rang. 'Stop!' it said, echoing from the city walls and the buildings all around. She saw the Skaven leader flinch, covering his pointed ears.

Across the square the crowds parted and a man strode through, moving with silent determination. But he was no Stormcast Eternal – he wore no helmet or armour, and carried only a wooden staff. The brim of his hat cast a long shadow, but the Shadowcaster's eyes still shone in the depths.

Kiri felt her knees weaken. As if a horde of stinking two-legged vermin wasn't bad enough, now this old wizard had to show his face. Maybe he was behind all this – he'd just given the Skaven an order, hadn't he? One that they had obeyed – the ratmen stood frozen, staring at the Shadowcaster with keen red eyes.

Then he raised his staff, jabbing it towards the Skaven. 'You... creatures have no place here,' he said, his voice tight with anger. 'Go now, or the consequences will be severe.'

Kiri watched him, surprised. What was happening?

Kreech smiled coldly, showing his teeth. 'Welcome, Shadowcaster. I have heard tales of your exploits, yes-yes. You are... shorter than I expected.'

The man did not even glance his way, casting a sharp gaze out across the courtyard. Kiri saw Kaspar struggling to his feet, his face smeared with coal

dust. He stood back to back with Alish
and Thanis, her steel gloves raised.

Kiri's catapult lay on the ground and
she reached for it, breaking free of
the claws holding her. The big Skaven
barely seemed to notice – he was
transfixed by the newcomer.

'I told you to leave,' the Shadowcaster
boomed, slamming his staff into the
stones. 'I will not say it again.'

Kreech laughed, a high-pitched
snorting sound. 'We hear you,
man-thing. But it is you who will leave.
In a box, yes-yes?' He raised his voice.
'Take him!'

The Skaven swarmed forward and
the Shadowcaster swung his staff,
dark wood flashing in the sunlight. He
swept it around in a wide arc and the
attacking line of Skaven were thrown
off their feet, tumbling and skittering
on the smooth stones of the courtyard.
Then he charged forwards, sending
startled Skaven spiralling into the air.

Kaspar, Alish and Thanis bunched

together as the Skaven resumed their attack. The Shadowcaster strode towards them, Skaven flying left and right as his staff swung and struck. The children ran to join him, and realisation flooded over Kiri like sunlight breaking through clouds. This Shadowcaster must be their master – what had they called him, Vertigan? He fought like a man with years of practice behind him, every move calculated, every blow forceful and on target. The Skaven didn't stand a chance.

Then a horn blew, and Kiri turned to see a phalanx of Freeguild soldiers marching into the square, forming a ragged, undisciplined attack line. Their helmets were too big and their breastplates too small, the fountains painted on their shields faded with age. But still they charged at the Skaven, waving blunt swords.

'Company, advance!' A barrel-shaped man rode at the rear, perched atop a snorting black stallion. He wore a flowing purple robe with gold trim, and the fountain on his helmet was topped with silver feathers. 'Remember your training!' he bellowed through bristly black moustaches. 'You are the Lifestone Defenders, Alarielle's chosen, and I am your lord. Together we will send these monsters back to the filthy holes they crawled from!'

He cantered forwards, wielding a keen-bladed sword. His soldiers advanced, their faces fearful but determined. The Skaven spun, facing this new threat. Kiri saw Kreech's jaw tighten.

And still the Shadowcaster moved through the fray, driving the ratmen ahead of him. Alish swung her hammer and Kiri heard a crash as a canvas stall toppled, pinning three Skaven beneath it. Thanis snatched up a Rhinox haunch and hefted it, taking out another two Skaven with the stump. Even the regular folk were starting to get involved – she saw several Duardin charging in with axes, and the young stallholder, Brodwin, swiping left and right with a dented copper pot.

Kreech stamped his clawed foot, letting out a string of curses. Then he raised his snout to the sky and cried out, 'Skaven, retreat! Fall back!'

The change was instantaneous. The ratmen fled, scrambling for the alleys leading out of the square. Kreech swept his cloak around him in a dramatic gesture, then he sprang back and was gone.

'That's right, you blaggards!' The Lord of Lifestone shook his fist at the fleeing ratmen. 'And if you ever show your snouts again, we'll deal with you just as roughly.'

He sat back on his horse, gripping the reins and sweating profusely. 'Now I've seen everything, by Sigmar. Real Skaven, just like in the stories. Here in my city.' Then his gaze fell on the Shadowcaster, and his eyes narrowed accusingly. 'Vertigan. Of course. Why do I suspect those creatures were looking for you?'

The man bowed his head. 'Lord Elias, I wish I knew. I've been trying to find out why they've come.'

The lord humphed. 'You just attract trouble. You and your little pack.' He squinted at Thanis and the others, as though looking for something, or someone. Then he wheeled his horse around, gesturing to his men. 'Back to the barracks! Double rations for everyone. We deserve it!'

Kiri turned her attention back to Vertigan and the others. Thanis was glaring at her furiously across the tangle of toppled stalls. 'Thanks for nothing,' she called out, and Kiri felt herself blush.

'We did okay,' Kaspar said, wiping the coal dust from his hands. 'We're all in one piece.'

'Barely,' the Shadowcaster said. 'I told you to find them, not fight them.'

'We did find them,' Alish said, clipping her hammer to her back. 'Then they sort of found us.'

'We found her, too,' Thanis said, gesturing at Kiri. 'We saved her then she tried to run away. She's a coward.'

Vertigan looked at her, leaning on his staff. 'Are you done running?' he asked. 'Will you come with us? We have food, and shelter. All you have to do is trust us.'

Kiri looked at him, his hand outstretched. The others grouped around, watching her silently. For a brief moment the urge to go with them was powerful. Then she remembered the promise she had made to herself, and stuck out her jaw. 'No,' she said. 'I'm leaving this city and I'm never coming back.'

She turned on her heel, moving towards the archway on the far side of the square. The rain lashed down, and now that the excitement was over she could feel the weariness in her bones, the weakness in her limbs. Where was she going to go? She could find shelter in the forest, most likely. But what about the wolves? And what was she going to eat? At that thought her stomach rumbled and suddenly she was famished, her head spinning.

She took another step, and another. The market was tilting around her and she wished it would stop; it was making her giddy. She tried to run but her legs wouldn't respond – all they wanted to do was rest. She felt them buckle under her, and she let out a

long, sighing breath as she slumped to
the ground.

CHAPTER FIVE

The Stone Fountain

Kiri surfaced slowly, rising through dark mist. She heard the drumming of rain on glass, and felt a deep ache in her limbs. Slowly, painfully, she opened her eyes.

She was lying on a narrow bed in a small room, the walls white and unadorned. A ragged blanket had been thrown over her, her cloak hung on the back of the wooden door. A high window let in a shaft of grey light, and craning her neck she could see low grey clouds and raindrops striking the glass.

A table stood at the bedside,

containing a glass of water and a bowl
of brown liquid. She dipped a spoon
and sniffed it – some kind of meat
soup, she guessed. It had gone cold, but
the smell was enticing. Her stomach
growled and she almost weakened, but
then she dropped the spoon, shaking
her head. She didn't know where she
was or why she'd been brought here.
She suspected those children were
responsible, and their master, the

Shadowcaster. But until she knew more, she wasn't about to trust anything they gave her.

She sat up. The door was most likely locked, but it didn't look that sturdy — a few good kicks and those rusty hinges might just break. Her boots lay on the floor beside the bed. She tugged them on, wincing at the ache in her muscles. She slipped on her cloak, checking that her catapult was still safe in the pocket. Then she stood, her head spinning. Her pulse raced as she stepped to the door, ready to knock it down if she had to.

She tried the handle. It turned smoothly and the door swung open. Kiri frowned. What sort of kidnapping was this?

Outside, a curving stone corridor ran from left to right. Stilling her breath, she listened. All she could hear was rain on the roof. But wait, was that a shout? A high, shrill sound, like laughter in the distance. Closing the door as quietly as she could, she moved in the opposite direction.

The hallway ended in a stone staircase, open to the sky. Looking down Kiri could see a large enclosed garden, with beds of earth arranged in a circular pattern around some sort of statue in the centre. Beyond the vine-covered walls rose a number of white towers, with peaked windows and winding stairways and cloud-shrouded minarets. To her right was a dome of coloured glass, all traced in black to form pictures – she saw silver peaks and golden turrets, the Magmadroths of the deep and the Stardrakes of the skies. This was the palace she'd seen on the hill, she was sure of it. It must be huge.

She crept down the steps, navigating by instinct. If she crossed this garden and through the building on the far side, she should be able to find a way back to the city. Then all she had to do was locate the market and the main gates, and leave Lifestone forever. She bit her lip. Somehow, she knew it wasn't going to be that simple.

She crept out across the garden, moving as swiftly as she could. There was a ring of trees in the centre and she ducked behind one, glancing around. There was no sign of movement, no sign of life. Actually, she thought, there was *really* no sign of life – from the shrubs to the flower beds to the trees that sheltered her, the entire garden was dead, just earth and stone and dry bark. Why would anyone keep a dead garden?

She hurried forwards, passing the statue. Except, she now realised, it wasn't a statue but a fountain, just like the one the Freeguilders had painted on their shields. But it was dry too, the open mouths of stone dragons, eagles and gryph-hounds mottled with dead moss. There were symbols carved around the fountain's bowl, grey runes that seemed strangely familiar. She circled the fountain, knowing what she'd find before she saw it – her own birthmark, cut into the stone. She touched it gently, and felt her wrist tingling. What was this place?

She crossed to the far wall, passing through an open doorway into another stone corridor, this one emptying into a large, silent hall with shuttered windows, the floor deep in dust. Beyond it was a cloistered yard, turrets looming over her as she slipped from one patch of shadow to the next. Another doorway, another corridor – and now, through a row of long windows, she could see out across sloping ground to the wall surrounding the palace, and beyond that... Her heart rose. The city, huddled under the grey sky. She was going to make it.

The passage led to a grand entrance hall with stone columns and a tiled floor, and a huge staircase leading up into the palace. There were murals painted on the walls and the arched ceiling – white-robed men and women, Aelves and Duardin, tending to the sick beneath the benevolent gaze of the Everqueen, Alarielle. Long-limbed tree-folk strode with armoured Stormcasts through wooded glades and between flowing fountains – again, she thought, more fountains.

But there, at the far end of the hall, was a door. It stood many times taller than Kiri herself, a slab of polished wood fixed to the wall with bolts thicker than her arm. But she barely registered these details because, to her delight, the door stood open, light streaming through. Beyond it she could see the gardens, and the wall, and Lifestone itself. She started forward, resisting the urge to sprint. She was almost there.

Then abruptly, she stopped. She didn't mean to; her legs just seemed to give up. She frowned, taking another step forwards. Except she didn't – her mind was telling her legs to move, but they

didn't want to comply. She reached out
with one uncertain hand, feeling for
an invisible barrier or magical wall.
Nothing. She took a sideways step then
darted forwards, trying to trick herself
into moving. But again she just stopped
dead, her feet refusing to go any
further. She cursed, frustration welling
up inside her. Why was this happening?

Then a voice spoke behind her, soft
and echoing in the gigantic entrance
hall.

'Leaving already?'

Kiri spun, her heart pounding. The
Shadowcaster descended the staircase,
his gaze fixed on her. His hat and
staff were gone and his eyes glittered
in his weather-beaten face. Behind
him came the others, Thanis and Alish
and Kaspar, and another boy that Kiri
didn't recognise, with dark eyes and
an open, inquisitive face. He carried a
long wooden staff topped with a roaring
lion's head carved in gold.

'You,' Kiri said, looking at Vertigan as

he crossed the hall towards her. 'I knew it.'

'Who else was it going to be?' Thanis whispered to the others, loud enough for Kiri to hear. They sniggered, and the Shadowcaster shot them a dark look.

'That's enough,' he said. Then he turned back to Kiri. 'Welcome to the Arbour, the centre of healing and learning for the City of Lifestone. Or at least, it used to be. My name is Vertigan, I'm the master here.'

'Stuff your welcome,' Kiri said. 'You kidnapped me.'

'We helped you,' Vertigan said. 'You were exhausted, you passed out. Thanis carried you up here, and Elio–' he gestured to the new boy, 'made you a soup full of healing herbs and strengthening roots.'

Elio blushed awkwardly. 'Did you like it?'

Kiri laughed. 'I didn't eat it. What kind of a fool do you think I am?'

Vertigan sighed. 'We're not trying to trick you, Kiri. I had you brought here because I need you to hear what I have to say. It's important. *You* are important.'

Kiri snorted. 'I'm nobody.'

'You are one of us,' Vertigan said. 'You bear the mark. As we all do.'

The Shadowcaster turned his arm over and there on his skin was a black rune: a simple arrow, with a featherless shaft.

'This is the mark of Ulgu,' he said, 'the Realm of Shadows. I wonder, how much do you know about the Mortal Realms, and Sigmar's war to liberate them from Chaos?'

Kiri thought of those mighty Stormcast warriors in the half-built keep. 'I know a bit.'

'Well, your own mark symbolises Chamon, the Realm of Metal,' Vertigan said. 'Which I suppose is why you're so steely and self-protecting.' He gestured to the others and they each stepped forwards, displaying their marks. 'Alish's birthmark is for Hysh, the Realm of Light. She's the brightest of us, an engineer and a great inventor. Elio's is for the realm in which we're standing, Ghyran, Realm of Life. He's a natural healer, he loves to see things grow. Kaspar's is the mark of Shyish, the Realm of Death and darkness. Explains why he's so quiet and sneaky, and such a good thief. And Thanis bears the mark of Aqshy, the Realm of Fire. A place of hot tempers and hard battles.'

'I've been there,' Kiri said. 'It's even rougher than she is.'

The tall girl snarled. 'Watch it.'

'Look, how is any of this possible?' Kiri asked, turning back to Vertigan. 'How can we share the same birthmarks?'

'Because we share the same destiny,' Vertigan said. 'Sigmar's war is far from over – the forces of darkness still rampage through the realms. Each of us must play our part to hold them back, even you, Kiri. You should be glad. You've been chosen for a very special purpose.'

Her eyes narrowed. 'What purpose?'

Vertigan shook his head. 'In time, child. Only when all seven are gathered together is the full truth revealed.'

'Seven?' Kiri asked. 'But I thought there were eight Mortal Realms?'

Vertigan nodded. 'Very good. The eighth is the dwelling place of Sigmar himself, the Celestial Realm of Azyr. No child could bear a mark so powerful.'

Kiri frowned. 'So you're looking for one more kid with the right birthmark?'

Vertigan nodded. 'And when I find them all will be revealed.'

Kiri sighed. 'So this could all be nonsense, couldn't it? You could be lying, trying to trick me.'

Alish shook her head. 'You felt the connection before, I know you did. He couldn't fake that.'

'And why would he want to?' Kaspar added. 'Why bring us together unless there's a good reason?'

Kiri faced them. 'In Hammerhal a sorceress tried to offer me a gold coin, but I wouldn't fall for it. Later I found out anyone who took them fell asleep and she boiled them for supper.'

Alish winced. 'That's horrible.'

'But Vertigan isn't a sorcerer,' Elio said, knuckles whitening on his long staff. 'Sigmar's beard, he's a great man. He took us in and helped us and—'

'And brought me here against my will,' Kiri snapped. 'And now he's using some spell to stop me leaving.'

'I placed wards around the palace to keep other things out, not to keep you in,' Vertigan said. 'The Skaven attacked in broad daylight – why would they be so bold? Something is happening, dark forces are moving against us and until I know who and why I need to keep the Arbour secure.'

'And keep me prisoner,' Kiri said.

Vertigan sighed. 'It's not safe out there. You saw the Skaven.'

'And you left us to be eaten by them,' Thanis muttered resentfully.

'I don't owe you anything,' Kiri snapped, clenching her fists. 'I can look after myself, I don't need protectors, I don't need friends and I certainly don't need some master telling me what to do. So *let me go*.' She stamped her foot on the tiles.

For a moment all was silent, then Vertigan sighed.

'Very well,' he said. 'I'm not in the habit of keeping anyone against their will. But you're taking a big risk.'

He raised his staff, muttering a string of strange syllables. Kiri felt the air shift somehow – she could feel a cool breeze through the archway, and hear sounds from the distant city. Gingerly she took a step towards the door, her eyes fixed on Vertigan and the others.

'If you run into trouble, you know where to find us,' the Shadowcaster called out, but Kiri shook her head. She could feel her birthmark tingling, almost burning, but she ignored it.

'I won't be coming back here.'

Vertigan shrugged. 'I wouldn't be so sure. This isn't over, Kiri. You have a part to play in this great war, mark my words.'

But she was already through the door, and running.

CHAPTER SIX

The Hooded Lady

Kiri fled across the sloping grounds, the rain beating in her eyes. The sky was dark, the clouds low. This had been another garden once – she saw bushes and bare trees in planted rows, their branches intertwined, their roots buried in the dead earth. The Arbour must have been a place of growth and healing, just like in the mural. But like the city it had faded, becoming a place of dust and death.

The defensive wall surrounding the Arbour was made of the same white stone as the building itself. But it was unlike any fortification Kiri had ever seen – instead of one smooth face it was carved into interlocking, almost human figures, facing away from the palace as though standing sentinel over the city. Their arms were linked, their torsos patterned with runic symbols in a language she'd never encountered.

In the centre one shape stood taller than the rest, stone legs apart to form an archway. A black iron gate had once blocked the passage but its hinges had rusted and the gate stood crooked, leaving a gap wide enough for her to squeeze through. Kiri took a deep, steady breath. She was out.

She crossed a wide cobblestone boulevard that ran across the front of the Arbour, turning into a long street leading straight downhill. The city lay sprawled on the hillside below her, ringed by the outer wall. The rain lashed down, the wind whipping at her sodden hair. The sun was lost behind the dense clouds.

Somehow she didn't feel as relieved

as she'd expected to. Those children had saved her life, she knew, back at the theatre. She smiled despite herself, remembering that thieving boy, Kaspar, shinning up the rope, and little Alish the inventor swinging her huge hammer. Thanis might be hard work but she was a real fighter, tougher perhaps than Kiri herself. And that healer, Elio, seemed like a decent kid, if a little awkward. Was she doing the right thing, leaving them behind?

Of course she was, she told herself. She barely knew them; she didn't owe them a thing.

And what of this Vertigan? The hooded lady's warning still echoed in her head: *he takes children...* Perhaps she was just repeating some rumour she'd heard. But what exactly were the Shadowcaster's intentions? Why had he brought them together, and why did they bear these marks? Kiri was no closer to understanding it than she had been before. But, she admitted

to herself, she didn't think Vertigan
was lying. Whatever his purpose, he
genuinely believed in it. And the others
trusted him.

She lifted her head and gave a
splutter of surprise. She'd been so
wrapped in her thoughts that she
hadn't paid attention to where she was
going – she'd just been following the
long downward street. Ahead of her
the road opened into a wide boulevard
running across-ways, and beyond was a
high wall of interlocking shapes, silent
under the grey sky. She was facing the
Arbour.

Kiri clutched her head. Losing her
way in narrow streets, running into
people she was trying to elude, those
had been unlikely but understandable.
But walking down a long hill only to
find herself back at the top, that simply
wasn't possible. Fear stabbed at her
heart. It had to be Vertigan working
some kind of magic, twisting her senses,
trying to keep her here. She balled her

fists. She wouldn't go quietly.

She turned and plunged downhill again, running as fast as she could while keeping her gaze firmly fixed on the city wall far below. Her muscles ached and the rain beat down, running into her eyes. She paused to wipe them and when she looked again the ramparts were gone. She was in a different street altogether, high-sided buildings closing her in.

Kiri struggled to breathe, her heart hammering. 'None of this is possible,' she said out loud. 'None of it.'

Why had her mother sent her to this dead city, this awful trap? But just the thought of Chetan made her bite back a sob, the memory of all she'd lost washing over her in a wave of grief and despair. She bit her knuckles, the dark street whirling around her.

'I did try to warn you.'

Kiri spun, surprise dispelling the clouds of panic. The voice had come from across the street, where pale light slanted through an open doorway. A figure stood there, her fine robe wrapped around her shoulders. Beneath the hood, Kiri saw a faint smile.

'I told you to stay away from him,' the lady admonished. 'That Shadowcaster. But you didn't listen.'

'I didn't get a choice,' Kiri said. 'He kidnapped me.'

'But you escaped. I'm impressed.'

Kiri sighed. 'I've been trying to get away but something's wrong. I keep losing my way.'

The hooded lady nodded. 'It's this place. It's... treacherous. Come inside, I can help.'

Kiri followed her to the doorway of what she now realised was the same apothecary's shop. Strange – she could've sworn it was down by the square, but this place was in the middle of a long, shuttered row. The air smelled sweet, like forest herbs and dried flowers. But beneath it all was a deeper scent, like cold, damp earth.

The walls inside the shop were lined with shelves stocked with bottles and beakers and copper alembics, many brimming with coloured liquids. Behind each shelf was a glass mirror, rows of them running right up to the ceiling. Peering into them Kiri saw herself reflected a thousand times, her bedraggled face repeated into infinity. Seeing movement in the glass she spun around, but there was nobody behind her. Just a shadow, she thought.

The hooded lady had crossed to the counter, where more bottles were arranged beneath a pane of glass. 'Can I interest you in something?' she asked. 'A salve for your bruises? Perfume to attract a special young man? A herbal charm to ward off bad spirits?'

Kiri leaned closer. She felt oddly distant, as if she were having a strange but not unpleasant dream.

'He took my son, you know,' the hooded lady said, her face suddenly serious. 'The Shadowcaster. Vertigan. He took my boy. Such a lively boy, so kind and gentle. His name was Kaspar.'

'I've seen him,' Kiri told her. 'He lives up there now. At the Arbour.'

'I've seen him too,' the hooded lady admitted. 'He doesn't laugh any more. Now he steals, and he fights, and when I try to speak to him he doesn't know me. Vertigan put a spell on him.'

'He tried to use magic to hold me prisoner,' Kiri told her. 'But I got out anyway.'

The lady smiled. 'You must be very strong to have resisted him.' Then she lifted her head and Kiri saw pale eyes glinting beneath the shadow of her hood. 'Will you use that strength to help me get my son back?'

'Of course,' Kiri nodded eagerly. 'If I can.'

The lady gestured to the counter. Lying on it was a small four-sided pyramid of black stone, with a hole bored in it. Something bone-white was encased inside; Kiri couldn't make it out.

'That pendant belonged to Kaspar,' the hooded lady explained. 'I feel like if he could see it again, if he could hold it, he might remember who he used to be. He might come back to me. Will you give it to him?'

Kiri bit her lip. 'I only just escaped. I don't want to go back there.'

'But you're so strong,' the hooded lady insisted. 'You fled once, surely you could do it again. And I can make sure you get out of the city. Look, I'll give you a map. You'll never be lost again.'

Beside the pyramid lay a sheet of folded paper with the words 'City of Lifestone' inscribed on the cover. Kiri hadn't noticed it before. She reached for it, then drew her hand back.

'I'm sorry,' she said. 'I have to leave this place. I promised myself.'

'But how will you find your way without a map?' the lady asked softly. 'You've tried several times, haven't you?'

'I'll just have to try harder,' Kiri said, the hairs on her neck beginning to prickle. She heard a strange rattling all around her and looked up to see the glass in the mirrors trembling. The room seemed darker, as though a veil had fallen. 'I should go, I really...'

'Stay where you are,' the lady said in a voice hard as ice, and Kiri felt her bones freeze. 'You'll do as you're told. And I'm telling you to *take that charm*.'

Sensing movement, Kiri looked down. Her hand was moving towards the table, entirely of its own volition. Panic bloomed in her chest as her fingers grasped the black pyramid, slipping it into her pocket.

'What's happening?' she demanded, her voice shaking. 'Please, stop.'

Dark shapes moved in the mirrors, writhing like smoke as the lady moved closer.

'I tried reason, but you wouldn't listen. So I had to take steps. Now you will run back to the Arbour and give

that stone to my boy.'

Kiri felt tears spring into her eyes. 'No,' she managed. 'I won't go back there. You can't make me.'

The lady laughed coldly. 'Child, I can make you do whatever I want. I can make you see things, anything I want you to see.'

Kiri looked around in terror. Spectral figures floated in the mirrors, their red eyes staring out. The bottles on the shelves were filled with black ichor, bubbling and spilling down the walls. On the counter, the map was just a scrap of tattered paper.

The lady seemed to glide over the carpet. 'I can do more,' she said. 'I can make you laugh, or sing, or cry until you're hoarse. I could make you pull out your own hair. Shall I?'

Kiri felt her hand twitch, saw it moving upwards in a sickly, jerking motion. She fought as hard as she could, feeling the birthmark blazing on her wrist. Her hand froze, vibrating as though caught between two powerful forces. Kiri focused all her strength, bolts of pain shooting up her arm. The hooded lady doubled her efforts, her will intensifying, forcing Kiri's hand up, and up. She was too strong, and Kiri heard herself cry out.

CHAPTER SEVEN

The Apparition

'Leave her be!'

Vertigan's voice boomed through the
doorway. Kiri reeled, and the lady's
power broke.

He strode into the shop, his staff
raised. The hooded lady turned to him,
her smile widening into a gruesome
leer. Vertigan took hold of Kiri, shoving
her towards the door.

'Go,' he cried. 'Now!'

Kiri staggered out into the street,
her mind reeling. Her strange dream
had turned to a nightmare; she felt
dazed and weak. But in the cold air

her thoughts found focus, her senses sharpening.

Vertigan stood facing his adversary. 'Who are you? What do you want with this girl?'

The hooded lady smiled sadly. 'Did I really mean so little to you, Mikal? I know it's been years but I expected you to recognise the girl to whom you pledged your undying love.'

Vertigan reeled as though he'd been struck. 'No,' he said. 'That's impossible.'

The lady reached up, drawing back her velvet hood. Her dark hair drifted in a halo around her porcelain face, and her features were perfect. Almost too perfect, Kiri thought – there was something barely human about the flawless balance of her thin lips and white eyes. She was like a doll, beautiful but lifeless.

Vertigan clasped one hand to his chest. 'You're dead,' he managed. 'Aisha Sand is dead.'

The lady nodded. 'The girl Aisha is

dead. The sorceress Ashnakh is very much alive.'

Vertigan flinched and Kiri started forwards, drawing her catapult. But he held out a shaking hand.

'Stay back. She's only an apparition, but she's still dangerous. She always has been.'

The hooded lady moved through the room and Kiri saw that he was right – her feet floated inches above the floor, her body passing through the counter as though it were nothing.

'I'm glad you remember,' she smiled.

Vertigan drew himself up, supporting himself on his staff and clasping his free hand over the birthmark on his wrist. He seemed to draw strength from it, and Kiri could feel her own mark tingling.

'How could I forget?' he asked. 'How could I forget the girl who destroyed everything I loved? Including herself.'

The lady smiled. 'All this time I've been waiting for you, Mikal. Waiting for you to bring them together, for the time to come again. You're so close. Just one more and the circle will be complete. And this time, you will fail utterly.'

Vertigan shook his head. 'You're wrong. These children are stronger than we ever were.'

'Are you sure?' the lady sneered. 'This one put up a fight, but it didn't take me long to break her.'

'Parlour tricks,' Vertigan spat. 'When

the time comes, they'll be ready. I'll make sure of it.'

The lady's eyes narrowed. 'You're old, Vertigan. Older than your years. Your strength is failing, while I grow more powerful every day.'

'But it's borrowed power, Aisha. That's all it ever was. Inside, you're the same lost child ready to do anything to make herself feel special, feel wanted, feel important.'

'You know *nothing*!' the lady roared suddenly, her apparition towering over him, her eyes shining with white fire. 'You are nothing. Just a weak old man surrounding himself with pitiful children. And you will feel my wrath.'

With a roar, dark shapes rushed from the mirrors, coiling like smoke into the room. The spectres were nebulous and unformed, red eyes glaring from howling clouds of black. They turned on Vertigan, writhing towards him. His robes fluttered and he leaned on his staff as though weathering a mighty storm.

'Perhaps I am just an old man,' he shouted over their ghostly wails. 'But at least I'm nobody's puppet.'

The lady screamed in rage. 'No, you are a slave. A slave to life, a slave to order, a slave to your precious King Sigmar and his pathetic followers. You will die, old friend. And these feeble children with you.'

She raised her hands, a ball of violet-coloured energy crackling around her fingers. With a cry she flung it at Vertigan, a perfect sphere of pure power rolling through the air. He tried to lift his staff to defend himself but the wraiths held him back, their ghostly forms coiling around his arms. The ball of energy struck him full in the chest and Kiri saw his mouth tighten in pain, his legs buckling.

The lady was already preparing another blast, weaving the power in her hands, her cruel eyes sparkling. Kiri stood powerless as the shapes wreathed around Vertigan's body, cackling with spectral laughter. The mirrors were dark, more of those hideous forms massing to attack. Suddenly, she knew what she had to do.

Kiri raised her catapult. The weight of it felt good in her hand. She slipped in a lump of shot and drew back the cradle, taking careful aim. The lady glanced at her and smiled cruelly.

'Oh, child,' she said sympathetically. 'You can't hurt me. I'm not even here.'

Kiri nodded. 'I know,' she said.

Then before her enemy could react she raised her aim, firing at the mirror above the lady's head. Her shot struck it dead centre, shards of glass exploding into the room, raining down through the startled apparition.

Kiri loaded again and took a shot, and another, and another. The mirrors shattered, the spectres wailing and weaving. Vertigan drew himself up, glancing back at Kiri, his face filled with weary gratitude.

The lady gave a high-pitched wail, her face seeming to fade as the mirrors broke. The apparition was failing, her shining eyes darting left and right. Vertigan took a step, glass crunching beneath his boots. His birthmark glowed red as he swung his staff at the spectres surrounding him, driving them off. They howled and thrashed, unable to hold their form without their mistress' influence. Soon all that remained was a tattered black fog. The lady gave a faltering cry, then she too was gone.

Vertigan staggered out into the street, his legs unsteady. Kiri ran to his side, taking his arm and holding him up.

'Who *was* that?' she asked, but the Shadowcaster shook his head, unable to speak.

'Someone I knew, long ago,' he managed at last. 'But she's gone now. Thanks to you.'

'How did you find me?' Kiri asked. 'Did you follow me?'

Vertigan nodded wearily. 'I had a feeling you'd run into danger, and if you did I might find out who was behind all this.'

Kiri smiled despite herself. 'So I was bait?'

Vertigan's face softened. 'In a manner of speaking. I was sure the Skaven couldn't be acting alone, and—'

'And you were correct, man-thing,' a voice hissed. 'Clever-clever.'

They spun around. A dark shape moved across the street, more than one, close to the ground and slinking silently closer. Then the clouds broke for a moment, and in the watery light the Skaven were revealed.

They moved in a silent swarm, ten of them at least, their fangs bared. Kiri drew her catapult as Vertigan's hand tightened on her arm.

'We have to get back to the Arbour. I'm too weak, I can't protect us here.'

Kiri nodded. She'd had no intention of going back, but what choice did she have? They backed along the street, eyes fixed on the approaching ratmen.

'Did you learn nothing last time?' Vertigan called out. 'You creatures do not belong here. Go back to your lairs and you will not be harmed.'

The Skaven began to laugh, a soft cackling in the shadows.

'Foolish man-thing.' Kiri recognised the rasping tones of the leader, Kreech. 'We are many, yes-yes. You are only two. We are quick-strong. You are slow-soft. We will bite. You will *die.*'

And with that the ratmen sprang forwards, their claws scraping on the stones. Kiri raised her catapult, loosing once, then again. Each time she heard a cry and saw one of the Skaven dropping back. But it wasn't enough.

'There's too many,' she said. 'We have to run.'

'Agreed,' Vertigan said, gesturing to an alley up ahead. 'That way. Stay close.'

Kiri ducked into the alleyway, Vertigan behind her, his face tight with exhaustion. He turned, swinging his staff up and back down, knocking one Skaven off its feet and smashing another to the cobbles. But his attacks lacked the swiftness they'd had in the square; he was weaker now, his encounter with the lady leaving him drained.

Then a shadow rose behind him and he tried to back away; too late. A huge armoured shape bore down, grabbing Vertigan's arms and forcing them against his sides. It had a snow-white pelt and razor-sharp claws, its meat-and-muscle body sheathed in rusty bronze armour. Vertigan bellowed in pain as the rat-thing sank its fangs into his shoulder. He was driven to the ground, the monster crashing down on top of him.

Kiri snatched a lump of shot from her pouch and took aim. But the creature's armour was too thick; the pellet ricocheted with a clang. The giant Skaven raised its head, its massive snout twitching horribly.

Kiri reloaded and drew the cradle back as far as she could, the wood groaning in her hand. Then she fired, right on target. The creature let out a shriek and fell back, clutching its crimson eye.

Vertigan staggered to his feet, wheezing with exertion. Kiri grabbed him and together they fled along the alley. Screams and screeches filled their ears, a clamour and clatter as the Skaven scurried in pursuit.

They burst into an open thoroughfare and her heart rose – ahead of them was the Arbour, those pale stone figures standing guard. She sprinted for the gateway, shoving through it. Vertigan followed then he turned back, raising his head to face the Skaven as they scuttled across the street. He raised his staff, weaving it through the air. Kiri could see the strain on his face, his birthmark glowing as he performed his spell. She felt the air shift, the voices of the Skaven becoming suddenly muffled, as though an invisible curtain had fallen.

The first of them charged at the gate, leaping with claws outstretched. Then it struck Vertigan's invisible wall and fell to the cobbles, shrieking in pain. Another tried but the spell was too powerful; there was no way for them to break through. The ratmen formed a ragged line in the street, raising their snouts to the sky and shrieking in anger. There were more of them, Kiri saw, another group emerging from the alleyway and joining the first.

'You cannot flee-flee, man-things!' Kreech screamed, his voice muffled behind the magical wall. 'We will come for you!'

Vertigan stood facing Kreech for a moment, his face ashen. Then he turned away. 'The Skaven is right,' he said quietly to Kiri. 'The wards won't hold forever. Come, we need to get inside.'

He leaned on her arm as they staggered across the silent grounds and back into the Arbour.

CHAPTER EIGHT

The Arbour

Vertigan led the way, guiding Kiri through the maze of hallways and corridors, courtyards and stairways. There was something unusual about this whole place, she'd noticed – the walls and arches weren't straight or angular; they seemed to flow naturally, with soft edges and gentle contours. Everything was made from wood or smooth stone, coloured in brown and green and soft grey. It was almost like being inside something living.

They came to a massive circular hall, with high white walls curving inwards. Overhead she saw that vast dome with its interlocking patterns of coloured glass. In the centre of the tiled floor two figures stood facing each other, clutching sturdy wooden sticks. Elio lunged forwards, swiping at Thanis as hard as he could. But the tall girl stepped back neatly, her first blow driving the stick from the boy's hand, her second knocking him flat on his backside.

'Sigmar's beard!' he cursed. 'You said you'd go easy this time.'

Thanis snorted. 'Life doesn't go easy. You reckon if we'd said pretty please, them Skaven would've just–'

She broke off, noticing Kiri and Vertigan. The stick dropped from her hand and she strode forwards, pulling Elio with her. 'Alish!' she cried out. 'Quick. Something's happened.'

Kiri heard the whirr of cogs and saw something descending from the ceiling – a small wooden platform suspended from ropes, with a figure perched on it. Alish hopped down, raising the ornate magnifying eyepiece strapped to her head and hurrying towards them. In the shadows behind her Kiri could see a large shape, something floating in the air beneath the dome. The shadows were too deep to make it out.

Vertigan drew himself up as the others approached, holding out a hand. 'There's nothing to be concerned about,' he said, but Kiri could hear the lie in his voice.

'What happened?' Elio demanded,

looking accusingly at Kiri. 'What did you do?'

'Nothing!' she replied. 'I left, and I ran, and then I... then I...'

She stopped, scratching her head. She couldn't for the life of her remember what had just happened. She recalled leaving the Arbour, and running down the hill. She'd met that mysterious lady... and then everything had started to blur. Vertigan had come, and after that the Skaven. But it was all so dim, like a dream that faded with the break of day.

'It wasn't Kiri's fault,' Vertigan insisted. 'The Skaven set upon us. But fear not, I've erected warding spells to keep them out.'

'How long will they hold?' Elio asked. 'Are we safe?'

'For now,' Vertigan told him. 'But I must rest. Get my strength back.' He moved towards a doorway in the far wall, from where golden light came streaming. Suddenly he staggered, leaning on his staff.

Elio ran to his side. 'Master, let me help you, I could make a strengthening potion, or—'

'Leave me be,' Vertigan snapped. Then his voice softened and he placed a gentle hand on the boy's shoulder. 'I'm just tired, Elio. In my absence, why don't you all show Kiri around the Arbour? Make her feel welcome.'

He entered the room, closing the door firmly behind him.

Elio stood open-mouthed. 'I... I've never seen him like that,' he said. Then he turned on Kiri. 'What happened out there?'

She racked her brains, trying to remember what had happened. Then she put a hand in her pocket, feeling something hard beneath her fingers. 'Wait,' she said, pulling out a small pyramid of black stone. 'I'm remembering a bit of it. There was a woman. She gave me this, to give to Kaspar. Where is he, anyway?'

Thanis shrugged. 'Probably in his

room. He likes to be alone.'

'Can you take me there?' Kiri asked. 'Maybe he'll know what it means.'

Thanis frowned. 'Me and Elio were busy training, in case you hadn't noticed.'

Elio gave a sigh. 'Vertigan says it's important we know how to defend ourselves, especially after today. Personally I'd rather heal people than hurt them.'

'You just need to toughen up,' Thanis laughed. 'And at least you know what ointments to put on your bruises after I kick your backside.'

'I'll take you to Kaspar,' Alish offered, shooting Kiri a shy smile. 'I can show you around the place as well, like Vertigan asked.'

Kiri nodded. 'I'd like that.'

Elio and Thanis retrieved their sticks, and the hall soon rang to the clatter of wood on wood. Alish took Kiri's hand, leading her across the hall under the dome.

'This is called the Atheneum,' she said. 'It used to be the main library. It's the biggest room in the Arbour, you can see it from every place in the city. And it's where I do my building.' She gestured to the walls and Kiri saw letters and numbers scrawled all over them in a fine, spidery hand. 'Those are my calculations,' Alish said proudly.

'What are they... for?' Kiri asked.

'To help with my inventions,' the girl grinned, then she pointed excitedly. 'Look, this is the latest thing I've been working on. Isn't it beautiful?'

In the space below the dome hung the dark shape that Kiri had glimpsed earlier, festooned with ropes. Squinting, Kiri now saw that it was a giant balloon made from canvas strips, a bulbous, rippling patchwork floating in mid-air. There was something suspended beneath it, a rickety wooden basket that had clearly been knocked together from anything Alish could find – the frame of an old arkenwood bedstead, part of a bookcase, half a wooden door. At one end the carved head of a gryph-charger rose like a ship's figurehead, while in the centre was a copper tank like a huge kettle, connected to a series of metal tubes.

'Did you make it yourself?' Kiri asked in amazement.

'Mostly,' Alish admitted. 'Elio helped with the stitching, and Thanis did the heavy lifting. Kaspar found me some of the parts, I didn't dare ask where he

got them. But it was my design. I like inventing things. And the Arbour is a great place for it – it's full of old junk and books on engineering and all sorts. I got the idea for the airship from a story Elio read out to us about the Kharadron. They're these Duardin who figured out how to fly.'

'I've seen their ships,' Kiri said. 'Not close up. Just in the distance.'

'Really, truly?' Alish asked, amazed. 'Please tell me.'

Kiri shrugged. 'They looked sort of like boats but with round things hanging at the top, like yours but smaller. And they had pennants streaming out behind, all flapping in the breeze.'

'They sound glorious,' Alish said dreamily. 'Well, maybe you can help me. I worked out how to make hot gas, with copper tanks and fire and different chemicals. But I think the Kharadron must have some special element they use to make their ships stay up – do you know anything about that?'

Kiri shook her head. 'Like I said, they were miles away.'

They left the hall and entered a long corridor, passing through a rainswept stone square and down a flight of winding steps, then into another corridor. It was lined on both sides with wooden shields, all painted with the fountain of Lifestone.

'This was the armoury,' Alish explained. 'The Arbour wasn't just about teaching and healing, there was a garrison here too. The Lifestone Defenders were great warriors once, according to Vertigan.'

Kiri thought of the hapless Freeguild soldiers she'd seen in the square. 'Must've been a while ago.'

'That's Thanis's room,' Alish gestured to a small wooden bolthole, the walls lined with Aelf-helms and Duardin hauberks, broadswords and scimitars, all polished to a fine gleam. On the floor was an upturned breastplate big enough to fit a giant, all heaped with ragged blankets. 'She actually sleeps in that, can you believe it?'

'Maybe it makes her feel safe,' Kiri said. 'What about Elio, where's his room?'

'He's a funny one,' Alish admitted. 'Me, Thanis and Kaspar are all orphans but Elio's father actually lives in the city somewhere. But as far as we can tell he never goes home – he just stays in the old healers' quarters brewing up stinking potions. It's a mystery.'

They passed through another arched doorway and into the daylight, dull and grey as the sun sank. They were in the garden Kiri had passed through earlier, the walls of the Arbour rising on every side, turrets scraping the clouds.

'This used to be the heart of the whole place, according to Vertigan,' Alish explained. 'The Lady Alarielle kept Lifestone hidden for most of the war, so when the worst of the fighting ended people would have somewhere to heal. This garden is where they'd come.'

'So what happened?' Kiri asked as they entered the circle of dead trees, their bare branches leaning inward.

Alish shook her head. 'No one seems to know. All we're sure of is that a few decades ago the whole city started to wither, and no one could stop it. All the teachers and the healers either left or found other callings.'

They approached the fountain, the runes carved around the rim. Kiri felt her birthmark tingling and saw that Alish was touching her wrist too. 'Whatever our purpose is, we're sure this fountain has something to do with it.'

They crossed to a flight of stone steps leading steeply downward. Now they were in the Arbour's basement, weaving through a labyrinth of sunken tunnels. Alish seemed to know exactly where she was going, navigating by shafts in the ceiling.

'That's Kaspar's room,' she said at

last, gesturing to a low doorway. A
sign was pinned to it, and as her eyes
adjusted Kiri could read the words
KEPE OWT printed in block letters.
'Why don't you see if he's inside?'

Kiri frowned. 'Are you sure? It does
say to "kepe owt".'

'That's just for strangers,' Alish said,
covering her mouth with her hand.
'He'll be glad to see you, honest.'

Kiri ducked uncertainly, peering inside.
All she could see was darkness.

'Hello?' she called. 'Kaspar?'

'Stick your head right in,' Alish said
encouragingly. 'He might be asleep.'

'Kaspar?' Kiri asked again. 'Are
you– Hey!'

Something exploded in her face and
she pulled back, spitting. She mopped
her brow with one hand and it came
back black with soot.

Alish hooted with laughter. 'I'm sorry.
But we've all done it. And you do look
funny.'

Kiri wiped her face with her sleeve.

'He lays *traps* for you?'

'They're not really for us,' Alish said. 'He just doesn't want anyone going in his room. You're lucky you didn't go any further, they only get worse.'

The doorway glowed and Kaspar appeared, a lantern in his hand. 'What's going on?' he asked. Then he spotted Kiri, her face black and her eyes narrow with fury. 'Oh. Sorry.'

'I made her do it,' Alish grinned. 'Think of it like an initiation. A welcome to the Arbour gang.'

Kiri glowered. 'I never said I wanted to be in the Arbour gang.'

'So why did you come back?' Kaspar asked. 'Did something happen?'

'Oh, right.' Kiri reached into her pocket, drawing out the black pyramid. 'I met a lady in the city who gave me this, for you. Does it look familiar?'

Kaspar took the pyramid, turning it over in his hands. 'I don't think so. Who was she?'

Kiri thought hard. 'I think she said

she was your mother. Is that possible?'

Kaspar shook his head. 'My mother's dead,' he said flatly. 'Whoever this was, it wasn't her.'

'I think Vertigan knew her,' Kiri said, squeezing her eyes shut. 'She... I think she did something to him. He was going to tell me more but the Skaven attacked.'

Kaspar's fists tightened. 'Wait, you saw the Skaven again? I think you'd better start from the beginning.'

Kiri told him as much as she could remember about their encounter with the ratmen and their flight to the Arbour. 'But Vertigan said we were safe. He put up warding spells.'

Kaspar frowned. 'But he also told you the spells wouldn't hold forever. And it sounds like he was pretty weak. I think one of us should keep watch.'

'I'll go,' Alish offered.

'We'll all go,' Kiri said. 'And if those Skaven look like they're up to anything, we'll fetch the others.'

They followed the underground tunnels beneath the Arbour, passing countless arches and doorways. Gusts of cold air made the torchlight dance, and Kiri felt herself shivering. But at last they climbed, emerging into a passageway leading to the main entrance hall. Through the doorway all was dark, the city slumbering under a black sky. Then the moon broke from behind the clouds, and Alish gasped in horror.

The street beyond the wall was a mass of moving shapes, countless Skaven swarming and screeching, their eyes and teeth like sparks in the moonlight. Kreech stood in the centre, his rotund companion at his side, both of them eyeing the Arbour hungrily. As Kiri watched, Kreech raised his hands, gesturing.

'Warlock!' he cried. 'Fetch my warlock!'

From the centre of the pack a skeletal Skaven appeared, rising above the others. But he wasn't taller, Kiri saw, not like that monster who had attacked

Vertigan. He was being held aloft, carried on the backs of other ratmen. He wore a close-fitting skullcap and swung a bronze censer, foul smoke gushing from it. He raised his bony hands and the ratmen fell silent, the warlock's rasping, wordless chant echoing from the Arbour's walls.

'That isn't good,' Kaspar said. 'They must be trying to break Vertigan's spell.'

'Can they do it?' Alish asked. 'I thought they were animals.'

The warlock lifted his voice, speaking more forcefully. Other Skaven took up the chant, their screeching cries drifting through the night air. Kiri felt their power building, the atmosphere crackling with it.

Then there was a rumble like thunder and the air seemed to clear, the lights of Lifestone growing suddenly brighter. The Skaven fell abruptly silent as one of them stepped forwards, reaching out cautiously and taking hold of the iron gate. He pulled it towards him and stepped through, squirming into the grounds.

He turned back to his fellows, giving a victorious cry. The Skaven raised their snouts and answered him, screeching and clamouring. Kreech raised a fist and Kiri gulped. Her blood was like ice in her veins.

Then the ratmen sprang forwards, shoving towards the gateway, clambering over each other in their haste to squeeze through the opening. Others began to scale the walls, leaping one upon the next, creating a hideous, living pyramid that swarmed higher and higher. At the base of the wall the ground began to erupt as the creatures tunnelled through from below, bursting out into the grounds and turning to face the Arbour.

Kiri shook her head, forcing herself to move. 'The door!' she shouted, taking hold of the massive wooden slab. It wouldn't budge. 'Help me, both of you!'

Kaspar and Alish joined her, heaving and straining. The hinges creaked and the door began to move, swinging into the archway. Kiri saw the Skaven springing up the steps, fangs bared and eyes flashing.

Then the door slammed shut.

CHAPTER NINE

The Battle

'It won't hold for long,' Kaspar said,
shoving the huge iron bolt across and
backing away.

'We need to find Vertigan,' Alish said.
'He's the only one who can stop them.'

'If he's strong enough,' Kiri said. Alish
looked at her in terror. 'I'm sure he
will be.'

They ran back through the maze of
stone corridors, their footsteps echoing.
They could hear glass shattering as the
Skaven smashed their way inside, then
a deep crash as the main door was
torn from its hinges.

At last the three of them crashed

back into the Atheneum, its walls bathed in coloured light. Thanis and Elio spun to face them, training staffs in their hands.

'They're here,' Kiri said urgently. 'They're coming.'

'Who's coming?' Thanis asked.

'Who do you think?' Alish cried.

Elio gave a cry of fear, running to Vertigan's door and hammering on it with his stick. 'Master!' he shouted. 'The Skaven!'

He banged again, but nothing happened – the hall was silent, just the whistle of the wind around the dome. Suddenly Kiri was convinced that Vertigan wasn't going to emerge, that the hurt he'd suffered was so severe that he would be unable to fight. What would she do if that happened? Would she stay and fight, even though she knew it was hopeless?

Then the door swung wide and the Shadowcaster emerged, his staff clutched in his hand. His face was still pale but he'd recovered some of his strength, and his voice was firm as he gathered them to him.

'Remember everything I've taught you,' he said. 'And whatever happens, stay together. We'll come through this, I promise.'

Kiri heard the scrape of claws in the hallway. The sound grew louder, chattering and clattering, screeching and shouting, until the Atheneum shook with the force of the Skaven's approach.

Vertigan leaned close, whispering in her ear. 'If I fall...' he began, but she pulled away, shaking her head.

'No,' she said. 'You won't.'

Vertigan grabbed her cloak, pulling her in. 'Yes,' he said. 'If I fall, you have to lead them. You've fought before, you can do it again. It'll be up to you to protect them.'

Kiri felt her stomach lurch. He was asking too much, placing too much responsibility on her shoulders. She wasn't even supposed to be here. She could still run, still flee before the Skaven arrived...

Then she saw Alish, looking up at her with scared, excited eyes, and Elio, his hands shaking where he gripped his training staff. Kaspar crouched with his hood up, poised and ready, and Thanis flexed her huge steel gloves, slamming them together with a metallic clunk. Kiri's thoughts flashed back to the market, that fateful decision to run away. She'd grown stronger since then, she realised. She wouldn't run again. This was her fight too.

Then the doors slammed open and the ratmen flooded through, red eyes bright in the multicoloured moonlight. Kreech stayed in the doorway, wringing his hands and cackling.

'Good, good!' he cried. 'Take them! Grab them! Capture them! Yes-yes!'

Kiri backed up, raising her catapult. Vertigan took a defensive stance, defying his enemies to come any closer. But there was weariness in his eyes

as he glanced towards Kiri, his gaze
speaking louder than words.

The others had bunched together,
facing outwards as the ratmen
approached. It was a strong defensive
position, but it would make them an
easy target as the Skaven rushed in to
surround them.

'Spread out,' Kiri said, gesturing
with both hands. 'Elio, hold the centre.
Kaspar, keep moving, don't let them pin

157

you down. Thanis, you're the toughest, take the fight to them if you have to.'

The tall girl glanced at her, the question *who put you in charge?* almost visible on her lips. But she bit it back, raising her gloves as the ratmen attacked.

Elio was the first to engage, the tip of his training staff driving into one of the Skaven and forcing the creature back. Alish unclipped her hammer, swinging it into the base of a nearby bookcase. The whole thing crashed down, flattening five furry bodies beneath it. Kaspar and Thanis held close together, the boy bobbing and ducking, tiring the Skaven out while the tall girl used her brute strength to drive them back.

Kiri pulled Alish to her. 'Is there anything up there that can help us?' she asked, jerking her chin towards the airship and the network of ropes and gantries surrounding it. 'Anything you can use?'

Alish thought for a second, then she grinned. 'I've got just the thing,' she said, running to the wooden platform. She tugged a rope and the platform rose, clear of the snatching claws of the Skaven.

'Elio, watch your back!' Kiri cried as four of the creatures lunged in to take hold of him. But Thanis was there ahead of her – she grabbed the foremost Skaven by the hood of its cloak, swinging it bodily into the other three. They toppled in a heap, the first Skaven tumbling out of its clothes, leaving Thanis clutching an empty robe. Kiri laughed, and Thanis shot her a proud grin. Then Kaspar popped up beside Thanis, snatching the Skaven cloak.

'Let me borrow this. I've got an idea.'

He ducked behind the fallen bookcase, but before Kiri could ask what he was up to there was a rumble beneath their feet, a violent tremor that set the walls rattling. It stopped abruptly, but by then Kaspar was gone.

Kiri turned her attention to Kreech. He had stayed clear of the fighting, preferring to direct from the rear. But now she saw him standing by the door to Vertigan's study, a slender, robed figure beside him – the Skaven warlock. They were talking together, tapping on the wood. Trying to break in? Yes, that had to be it.

She wanted to call to Vertigan, to warn him what was happening. But he was in the eye of the storm now, his staff sweeping and lunging, thrusting and parrying, a wall of fallen Skaven piling up around him. He was visibly weakening, Kiri saw, his reach narrowing, his pace slowing. And more Skaven were still swarming in, clambering over their own wounded in their eagerness to join the fray. They'd have to take care of this themselves.

'With me!' she cried out, putting as much force into her voice as she could muster. 'Come on, let's show these hairy villains what happens when you mess with our city. For Lifestone!'

'For Lifestone!' Thanis cried in answer, slamming her gloves together and charging forward, driving a wedge through the mob of ratmen. Kiri followed, loosing her catapult over Thanis's shoulder, taking one of the creatures down.

Then a shrill shout cut through the clamour, and Kiri looked up.

'Everybody duck!' Alish cried, putting her head out of the airship's basket. Something blazed in her hand, the flames reflected in her wild, wide eyes. 'For Azyr!' she shouted, hurling the flaming object towards the study.

There was a deafening bang, and clouds of pitch-black gas came gushing out. The warlock tumbled back, his ceremonial cap toppling free as he tripped over his own feet. Kreech vanished in the smoke, but Kiri could hear him coughing and spluttering.

'Black-black!' Kreech wailed. 'I'm blind! Bliiiiind!'

Kiri dived into the smoke. Her eyes stung and she could see almost nothing, but Kreech made such a clamour that she couldn't miss him, raising her catapult as the smoke cleared. He stared back at her, tears streaming down his furry cheeks.

'Get out,' Kiri ordered, taking steady aim. 'Leave this place. There's nothing for you here.'

Kreech bobbed his head, grinning grotesquely. 'Wrong-wrong, girl-thing,' he hissed. 'Behind this door are many goodies, many delightful things. You can share them if you—'

'She said go,' Thanis growled as she stepped up beside Kiri, her gloves raised.

'And she meant it, by Sigmar,' Elio added, raising his training staff.

Kreech backed up, looking at them each in turn, weighing his chances. Then a grey-robed Skaven ran to his side, face hidden beneath a bronze helmet. It tugged its master's wrist but Kreech shook it off.

'Not now, fool-fool,' he spat. 'Can't you see I'm–' His eyes widened.

The robed Skaven held a short sword, pointed at the packlord's chest. 'We told you to leave,' it said, lifting the visor. Kaspar's eyes were dark beneath the brim. Kiri was amazed – the boy had moved just like a Skaven, hunched and scurrying.

Kreech gulped, looking down at the sword. Kiri thought she saw a crafty look flash across his face, but it was gone as quickly as it came.

'Yes-yes,' he said. 'Good-good man-things, we will leave.' He lifted his gaze. 'Back-back!' he shouted, waving his arms and backing to the door. 'Enough gnawing! Enough fight-bite! Skaven, retreat!'

The ratmen did as they were told, streaming through the archway leaving destruction in their wake. Furniture had been flattened, bookcases toppled.

They dragged their fallen with them, leaving a trail of discarded armour and tattered cloaks. Vertigan was revealed in the centre of the room, his face streaming with sweat and grime, his hands shaking where they clutched his staff.

Elio ran to the doorway, shaking his fist and yelling.

'That's right! And don't even think about coming back!' He turned to the others, grinning. 'I don't believe it. We won. They're gone!'

Kiri shook her head. 'I don't believe it either. I don't trust that Kreech as far as I could throw him.'

'Vertigan, what do you think?' Alish asked.

But the Shadowcaster was staggering, his face a mask in the moonlight. He sank to his knees, clutching his birthmark. His breath came raggedly and there was blood on his hands.

Elio hurried towards his master. But

before he could reach Vertigan's side that unearthly rumbling came again, and the floor of the Atheneum shook. Elio froze, looking around. Vertigan lifted his head, but Kiri could see that he was done. Whatever was coming, he wouldn't be able to fight it.

The ground trembled violently and Kiri put her hands out, struggling to maintain her balance. There was a rending creak and the floor split open, a long, jagged seam running from one side of the Atheneum to the other. The crack widened as though an earthquake had struck. Dust erupted from it.

Then the flagstones around Vertigan shattered and small shapes began to boil out – hundreds, thousands of them, screeching and clawing. Rats, an army of them, swarming over the Shadowcaster as he strove to beat them back. He grabbed his staff but it was no use, the creatures were too small and too quick, streaming over him in a filthy black tide.

The floor dropped, a sinkhole opening in the centre of the room. And Vertigan tumbled into it, the rats tugging at his clothes, dragging him down into the dark. Elio flung himself forwards but the rats massed, teeming towards him, clambering up his legs and over his feeble, battering hands. Thanis pulled him back, watching as they swarmed back to the ragged hole. Kiri caught a last glimpse of Vertigan's face, then he was gone.

CHAPTER TEN

Witch Hunter

'No!' Elio screamed, sprinting to the rim of the ragged hole that had opened in the middle of the floor. He coughed dust, tears streaming down his face. Kiri ran to join him. She could see nothing, just earth and darkness. There was no sign of the rats, and no sign of Vertigan.

'Wait, you don't–' she cried, but Elio had already jumped. He dropped a short distance, landing in a crouch. The hole was angled, a short, sheer drop then a branching, almost horizontal passage. Elio scrambled inside, letting out a cry of bewilderment.

'It stops,' he said. 'It just stops! Where have they gone?'

Kiri dropped into the sinkhole. Elio was right: the tunnel ran smoothly forward for a short distance, then came to an abrupt end.

'Sigmar's beard, people can't just vanish,' Elio moaned. 'It's magic. It has to be magic. But there must be a way to get him back.'

'How?' Kaspar asked, peering over the edge. 'None of us do spells.'

'What about Vertigan's study?' Alish asked, gesturing back towards the room. 'The Skaven certainly seemed eager to get inside – maybe there's something in there that can help.'

'Vertigan's room is private,' Elio said. 'He's never let us go in there. Even me, and I'm his favourite.'

Thanis looked at him doubtfully, but she let it go. 'It's an emergency. He'd understand.'

But when they crossed to the study they found that the door was still firmly locked. There was a single keyhole in the centre, surrounded by a bronze disc printed with a series of symbols.

Kaspar crouched, taking a pouch from beneath his robe and opening it to reveal an array of metal implements: picks, files and blades. He peered into the keyhole, inserting one tool after another. Moments passed.

'Is this going to take long?' Elio asked at last. 'Sigmar only knows what those creatures are doing to him.'

'It's not working,' Kaspar said, frustrated. 'I can't get a grip. It's like no lock I've ever seen.'

'Move,' Thanis said, pulling him to his feet. 'Out of the way.'

'No, wait,' Elio protested. 'I don't think that's a good...'

She slammed the door with her shoulder but it barely even shook. She hit it again, and again, but the study door stood firm. Thanis cursed.

'Must be some kind of spell on it.'

'Or you're just not as strong as you think,' Elio muttered.

Thanis turned on him. 'What did you say?'

Kiri stared at the door, trying to block out their bickering voices. There had to be a way inside, some secret method that would bar anyone that Vertigan deemed unworthy. Who would he trust enough to let in?

She looked again at the wheel surrounding the lock. The symbols printed on it looked familiar – they were realm-marks, she realised, the same ones they all bore. Could it really be so simple? She reached up, pressing her birthmarked wrist against the lock. There was a click and the door swung open.

'Hey,' Alish was saying, 'let's all stop arguing and figure out how to– Oh.'

Light flooded over them from a lantern hanging inside the study. Cautiously, Kiri stepped inside.

From floor to ceiling the little

room was lined with books – heavy tomes, most of them, bound in black leather. There were also rows of cases containing artefacts of every conceivable shape and source: Duardin jewellery and Aelfish scrolls, ancient weapons and sacred armour, statues of beasts and men and warriors. In the centre was a large desk, its surface scattered with maps and charts, paper and quills and pots of ink.

'Who *is* this master of yours?' Kiri

asked, taking it all in. The preserved skull of a great horned manticore leered down from the wall, its glass eyes gleaming in the light.

'He's a healer,' Elio said, stepping in.

'And a teacher,' Alish added.

'And I think he was a soldier, once,' Thanis put in.

'He's a witch hunter,' Kaspar said, and they turned in surprise. 'None of you knew? I thought it was obvious.'

'But witch hunters are creepy,' Alish protested. 'They're all dark and brooding and tough.'

'What, like Vertigan?' Kiri asked.

'Yes, but...' Alish said. 'But he's nice, too.'

'He's a member of the Order of Azyr,' Kaspar said. 'It's this ancient society dedicated to Sigmar. There were more of them here once, scholars and soldiers and warrior-priests. Along with the lord's battalions they guarded the Arbour so the healers and the teachers could do their work.'

'So where did they all go?' Elio asked. 'And why did Vertigan stick around?'

Kaspar shrugged. 'I haven't been able to find out. It's not like Lifestone is teeming with witches to hunt.'

Kiri thought of the hooded lady, and wished she could remember what had happened. She looked up at the shelves, shadows leaping in the light of the lantern.

'We should start by trying to find out something about the Skaven,' she said. 'Anything that could help us figure out where they might have taken h–'

'Like this?' Thanis asked. Right there on the desk a book lay open, filled with scrawled words and fierce illustrations depicting the ratmen in combat. She shoved it towards Elio. 'Read it.'

He looked at her quizzically. 'I thought Vertigan was giving you lessons.'

Thanis blushed. 'He is. But I have trouble with the big words.'

Elio leafed through the book. 'This is Vertigan's own journal. His observations and private thoughts. I don't know if...'

'Just read,' Thanis insisted.

Elio traced his finger down the page. 'These recent entries seem to focus on the Skaven. I guess they were in his thoughts since those sightings down by the theatre. He says they must be entering the city through gnawholes, bridges between realms created by their most powerful warlocks. These temporary Realmgates allow them to surprise their enemies, extract captives...'

'That's it,' Alish said. 'They took him through one of those holes.'

'A Realmgate,' Elio said in awe. 'Right here in the Arbour.'

'Can we follow?' Thanis asked.

'There are few ways to follow a Skaven once he has retreated through his gnaw-hole,' Elio read aloud. 'Most are known only to the greatest wizards – well, that's not us. An artefact called the Light of Teclis was created by the sorcerer Accore during the Hyshian raids, and several examples are known to have survived the ravages that followed. It's possible one could have made its way to the Arbour. I must conduct a thorough search.'

'Well?' Thanis asked, looking around. 'Has anyone seen this... Light of Tick-Tock?'

'Teclis,' Elio corrected her.

Kiri inspected the illustration in Vertigan's book. The Light was a jagged black cylinder set with a white stone.

'Kaspar, you've explored this whole place,' Alish said, turning. 'Have you seen this—'

She broke off, looking around. There was no sign of the boy – Kaspar had simply disappeared. He must have slipped away while we were talking, Kiri thought. A little odd, but then he was an odd kid.

'Well, that's great!' Elio sighed. 'Vertigan's gone, now Kaspar's disappeared too.'

Thanis shrugged. 'Maybe he's gone off to find this Light of Tealeaf thing.'

'*Teclis*,' Elio snapped.

'I know,' she grinned. 'That time I just did it to annoy you.'

Elio turned red. 'This isn't the time for stupid jokes.'

Thanis scowled. 'Are you calling me stupid?'

'I don't think he was,' Alish put in, holding up her hands. 'He just said—'

'I don't need you to stick up for me,' Elio shouted. 'I can speak for myself.'

'Don't yell at her!' Thanis barked. 'She's just trying to—'

Kiri's patience snapped. 'HEY!' she roared, climbing up on Vertigan's chair, and from there onto the table. She could feel her cheeks turning red, her fists trembling as she looked down at their startled faces.

'Enough, all of you,' she said. 'We don't have time for any of this. Elio's right, we have to get Vertigan back. But to do that we need to work

together, just like we did in the
Atheneum. We might not know why we
have these marks, but we're a team
now whether we like it or not. So we
need to start acting like one. Agreed?'

They looked at her, mouths open.

'Good. Now, Thanis and Elio, go and
make absolutely sure the Skaven are
gone. Alish, find Kaspar and see if he's
seen this Light thing anywhere. Take
the book so you can show him the

picture. If not we'll begin a search just like Vertigan was going to do, split up and cover this whole place from top to bottom.'

Elio opened his mouth to protest, but a sharp look from Kiri made him shut it again.

'I know, it'll take time. But we need a plan, and this is the best we've got. Vertigan's counting on us, so let's just–'

'Wait!' Alish said suddenly. She was squinting at the drawing of the Light of Teclis through her magnifying eyepiece, inspecting it from all angles. 'I didn't look at this properly before, but now that I have, it kind of... I might be wrong, but it sort of...'

'Say it!' the others demanded in unison.

'Well, it looks *just* like the thing I've been keeping my spare screws in.'

REALMS ARCANA

PART ONE

THE MORTAL REALMS

Each of the Mortal Realms is a world unto itself, steeped in powerful magic. Seemingly infinite in size, they contain limitless possibilities for discovery and adventure: floating cities and enchanted woodlands, noble beings and dread beasts beyond imagination. But in every corner of every realm, a war rages between the armies of Order and the forces of Chaos. This centuries-long conflict must be won if the realms are to live in peace and freedom.

AZYR

The Realm of Heavens, where the immortal King Sigmar reigns unchallenged.

AQSHY

The Realm of Fire, a region of mighty volcanoes, molten seas and flaming-hot tempers.

GHYRAN

The Realm of Life, where flourishing forests teem with creatures beyond counting.

CHAMON

The Realm of Metal, where rivers of mercury flow through canyons of steel.

SHYISH

The Realm of Death, a lifeless land where spirits drift through silent, shaded tombs.

GHUR

The Realm of Beasts, where living monstrosities battle for dominance.

HYSH

The Realm of Light, where knowledge and wisdom are prized above all.

ULGU

The Realm of Shadows, a domain of darkness where dread phantoms lurk.

REALMGATES

The only way to travel between the eight Mortal Realms is through a Realmgate, a magical portal torn in the fabric of space. Realmgates can take an infinite number of forms – they might appear as a mystical door or

opening, a ferocious storm or a bolt of lightning, an endless stairway or bizarre magical artefact, even a person or a living creature. But

they are very rare and very precious – whoever controls the Realmgates controls the Mortal Realms themselves.

STORMCAST ETERNALS

Immortal warriors in the struggle against Chaos, the Stormcast Eternals are King Sigmar's finest warriors. Heroic champions, the Stormcasts were reforged in the fires of Azyr, clad in sigmarite armour and sent out into the Mortal Realms to confront the enemies of Order. They appear in a flash of lightning, plunging straight into the heart of battle where their strength is needed most.

SIGMAR

The immortal King Sigmar leads the forces of Order against the warriors of Chaos. Wielding his legendary hammer Ghal Maraz, it was Sigmar who first began the battle to liberate the Mortal Realms, bringing light and wisdom and freeing countless peoples from oppression. From his celestial realm of Azyr, Sigmar dispatches his Stormcast Eternals into battle, fighting ceaselessly to drive back the forces of Chaos.

DARKOATH BARBARIANS

Just one of countless brutal tribes who roam the Mortal Realms, the Darkoath Barbarians are pledged to the forces of Chaos. Clad in leather and metal armour adorned with the skulls of their vanquished foes, these savage marauders cause mayhem and misery wherever they go: plundering and pillaging. Only the armies of Sigmar have the strength to stand against them.

Darkoath Barbarians often fight alongside captive Troggoths – grotesque, troll-like creatures many times the size of a man.

KIRI

Bearing the mark of Chamon, the
Realm of Metal, fourteen-year-old Kiri
is as strong and steadfast as steel.
Raised in the barbarian slave camps of
Aqshy, Kiri learned to fight as soon as
she could walk, honing her skills with
a catapult. Somehow, this harsh life
hasn't made her cruel or resentful –
Kiri is honest, stout-hearted and brave.
But she does find it hard to trust other
people, preferring her own company to
that of a group.

VERTIGAN

Known to the citizens of Lifestone as the Shadowcaster, mysterious grey-haired loner Mikal Vertigan is master of the Arbour. For decades he lived there alone, but in recent months he has been gathering a band of young apprentices, teaching them how to fight and defend themselves. His purpose in this mission remains unknown, but all of the children are known to bear a particular birthmark – black runes symbolising seven of the eight realms (no mortal could bear the mark of celestial Azyr). In fact, Vertigan bears one of these marks himself – the rune of Ulgu, the Realm of Shadows. It's an appropriate symbol for this secretive, enigmatic man.

THE SKAVEN

The Skaven are a race of vicious humanoid ratmen famed for their greed, cunning and peculiar manner of speech. Cruel and cowardly when encountered alone, the Skaven's power lies in their vast numbers: no one knows how many millions there are across the realms, but they spread like a plague and consume everything in their path. They live in vast, trackless earthen warrens and their clans are led by packlords, who tend to be a little smarter and more ruthless than the common Skaven clanrat.

LIFESTONE

The city of Lifestone lies in Ghyran, the Realm of Life, between the Everlight River and the Houndstooth Mountains. Once a thriving metropolis under the protection of Alarielle the Everqueen, the city has now fallen into disrepair – though few of its citizens understand why. They tend to be a sullen and unfriendly lot, selfish and resentful of outsiders. And the city itself is equally unwelcoming: its roads are narrow and winding, its buildings dark and ramshackle.

Prominently placed above this nest of streets is the Arbour, a palace of white towers crowned with a coloured dome. Once it was the centre of healing and learning for the whole of Lifestone; now it's as faded and crumbling as the rest of the city.

ABOUT THE AUTHOR

Tom Huddleston is an author and freelance film journalist based in East London. His first novel, future-medieval fantasy *The Waking World*, was published in 2013. He's since penned three instalments in the official *Star Wars: Adventures in Wild Space* series and is also the writer of the *Warhammer Adventures: Realm Quest* series. Find him online at www.tomhuddleston.co.uk.

ABOUT THE ARTISTS

Magnus Norén is a freelance illustrator and concept artist living in Sweden. His favourite subjects are fantasy and mythology, and when he isn't drawing or painting, he likes to read, watch movies and play computer games with his girlfriend.

Cole Marchetti is an illustrator and concept artist from California. When he isn't sitting in front of the computer, he enjoys hiking and plein air painting. This is his first project working with Games Workshop.

An Extract from book two
Lair of the Skaven
by Tom Huddlestone
(out May 2019)

'Good-good man-things!' the Skaven stammered, clutching the rune-covered staff and retreating fearfully. 'Nice, gentle man-things, have mercy on a poor, pitiful Skaven, yes-yes!'

Elio stepped forward, backing the furry, fanged rat-creature into a corner. 'Why should we show mercy? You showed none when you invaded our home and tried to kill us.'

'Or when you kidnapped our master,' Thanis added. She was covered in bruises and her red hair was a wild tangle. 'That's his staff you're holding. I suggest you give it back before I take it from you.'

Hundreds of Skaven had attacked the Arbour the night before, swarming through the palace and taking the five children and their master Vertigan by surprise. They'd managed to drive the creatures back, but then the Skaven leader Kreech had sent rats to burrow up through the floor and snatch Vertigan from right under their noses. He was dragged through a mystical gnaw-hole between the realms, leaving his staff behind. And now they'd caught this creature trying to sneak off with it.

The Skaven bowed, holding out the staff. Thanis snatched it. 'Now please-please,' the creature whimpered pitifully. 'Let this poor-poor vermin go.'

'Not yet,' Kiri said, holding up a hand. She was the newest member of the group, and Elio still wasn't sure he trusted her. She and Vertigan had

had some kind of encounter yesterday, a run-in with a mysterious hooded lady that had left their master too weak to repel the Skaven when they attacked. Kiri claimed she couldn't remember everything that had happened.

'If you give us information,' she said to the creature, 'we'll consider letting you go.'

Its black eyes narrowed. 'What sort of information, girl-thing?'

'Where have you taken our master?' Elio asked.

'What's through that realm-hole... thing?' Thanis added.

'Who is this Kreech, and why did he come after us?' Kiri finished.

The Skaven's lips drew back over slavering fangs – it was smiling, Elio realised. 'Kreech is our Packlord, servant of the Great Horned Rat and leader of the Clan Quickfang. And your master is safe-safe in our warren, you will never see his ugly man-thing face again.'

'Where is this warren?' Elio asked. 'Through the gnaw-hole? How many Skaven are on the other side?'

'Many thousands,' the creature grinned. Then a thought occurred and it shook its head hurriedly. 'No, few-few. Not many at all.'

Thanis threw up her steel-gloved hands. 'It's just saying whatever comes into its head.'

'Why did Kreech take our master?' Elio demanded. 'What makes him so special?'

The Skaven cackled. 'Kreech does not need me to know these things. He only needs me to fight-bite!' And he ducked his snout, shoving into Elio and trying to flee.

Elio stumbled as the creature slammed past him, baring its fangs. But Thanis swung low with Vertigan's staff, knocking the Skaven off its clawed feet and sending it tumbling across the tiled floor. It lay dazed for a moment, then it scrambled towards the door.

'Get back here,' Thanis growled, lunging forward. 'You miserable little—'

Kiri took her arm, holding her back. 'Let it go. We've got enough to worry about, and like you said it'll only tell us lies.'

Elio picked himself up, brushing his tunic. Then he reached out to take the staff from Thanis. 'Vertigan would want me to have it,' he said. 'I was his apprentice, after all.'

Thanis's eyes narrowed. 'You were, were you?' she asked doubtfully. Then she sighed and handed it over. 'Makes no difference to me.'

They turned back to the centre of the old library, where the little inventor Alish crouched beside the sinkhole that the rats had chewed in the floor, the one they'd dragged Vertigan down into. She was studying the Light of Teclis — a gauntlet-shaped artefact crafted from black metal, with a white moonstone set into the centre. They'd learned of its existence from Vertigan's personal journal, a large, dusty tome that Alish held in her free hand. The book had explained how powerful Skaven mystics were able to chew holes in the fabric of reality itself, opening gates between the realms. The Light of Teclis could reopen the gnawhole, allowing non-Skaven to pass through. Or at least it was supposed to, if only they could figure out how it worked.

'Let me try,' Elio said, taking the device from Alish and studying it closely. Vertigan's book explained all about the rat-men and how they lived, but it said nothing about how the Light of Teclis actually operated. Elio pointed the central moonstone down into the gnawhole and concentrated as hard as he could. Nothing happened.

'Maybe you need to say an incantation,' Thanis suggested.

'Or maybe you need to be a witch

hunter to wield it,' Alish said, echoing
Elio's own fears. That was the other
important fact they'd learned last
night – all the time they'd known
him, Vertigan had secretly been a
member of the Order of Azyr, an
ancient society in service to Sigmar
and committed to rooting out evil
across the realms. Elio didn't know
why the master had never taken him
into his confidence, he would've kept
the secret safe, even from the others.
But now Vertigan was gone, and Elio
didn't have the knowledge or expertise
necessary to get him back.

'Or maybe it's just useless,' he said,
slipping the Light from his hand. 'May
as well just chuck it in the–'

'Wait,' Kiri said. 'Let me try
something.' She took the device from
him, climbing down into the gnawhole.
She gripped the gauntlet, then with
her free hand she touched the mark
on her wrist, the black rune that
each of them bore a version of, even

Vertigan. These birthmarks symbolised the different realms, all except for Azyr, whose power was too great for any mortal to bear.

Kiri shut her eyes, squeezing tighter. Elio felt a vibration in the air, like a whisper just beyond the limits of his hearing. The pages of the book ruffled silently, then a beam of white radiance burst from the moonstone, lighting up the sides of the tunnel.

Kiri gasped in amazement. 'It's working!'

Alish grinned. 'Incredible!'

Kiri held her arm steady. 'I saw Vertigan drawing strength from his mark last night,' she said. 'So I thought maybe...'

Elio touched his own birthmark. He didn't feel any kind of power, he never had. But the marks had drawn them together, had led all five children to the Arbour, and to Vertigan. Clearly there was more to them than he'd ever suspected.

He dropped to the edge of the sinkhole, slipping in beside Kiri. 'Let me try.'

He held the device, gripping his birthmark with his free hand. He felt a tingling beneath the skin, a sense of power radiating along his arm. The Light of Teclis seemed to tremble infinitesimally, sending vibrations up into the central moonstone. Then a pale light emerged from it, a narrow beam in which tiny motes of energy gathered and span.

Elio crept forward, training the Light on the end of the tunnel. He took another step, and another, and suddenly he saw that his arm had disappeared up to the wrist, now the elbow. 'Look!' he said. 'It's working! Come on, follow me!'

He started forward but a firm hand on his shoulder stopped him. 'Wait,' Kiri said. 'We've got no idea what's on the other side. We need to think before we do anything.'

'What's to think about?' Elio demanded. 'Vertigan's through there. We need to him back. That's all that matters.'

'But there could be a thousand Skaven on the other side,' Alish said, dropping beside Kiri. 'There could be vampires or orruks or a lake of fire, or anything else horrible that you can imagine.'

'Stay here, then,' Elio snapped. 'Stay where it's safe. But I'm going, with or without you. Vertigan gave us purpose, he made our lives mean something. He protected us, now we have to do the same for him.'

'We could use these.'

Kaspar squatted on the edge of the sinkhole, eyes bright beneath a grey hood. He had wandered off last night, right around the time they found the book. Elio wondered where he'd been, but this wasn't the time to ask.

Kaspar held up a pair of cloaks, ragged and torn at the seams.

Elio recognised them – Skaven robes, presumably torn off during the fighting. 'There are all sorts of helmets and bits of armour up here as well,' Kaspar said. 'Should make decent enough disguises.'

Elio grinned. 'That's perfect. We'll sneak through and see what we can find out.'

'And what happens if they catch us?' Alish asked. 'What happens if we're not sneaky enough?'

Thanis dropped into the hole, laying a hand on her shoulder. 'I'll look after you,' she said. 'But Elio's right, we have to go after Vertigan. He'd do it for us, wouldn't he? And besides, I've quite started to enjoy thumping Skaven. Their fur's nice and soft.'

Kiri nodded too. 'I agree. We may not know everything about Vertigan's mission and our own purpose, but we know it was important for the city, maybe for the realm. He was a soldier in the war against Chaos, and it's our time to fight too. Alish, you can always stay behind if you–'

'No,' Alish sighed, wringing her hands. 'I want to get him back as much as any of you.'

Kaspar put a hand on her shoulder. 'I'm scared too. Like, *really* scared. But as long as we're together, I think we'll be okay.'

Alish placed her hand on his, and seemed to take strength from it. She nodded firmly.

'We're agreed then,' Elio said. 'Let's round up some disguises. Oh, and it's going to be dark down there, maybe we should think about bringing a tinderbox of some kind.'

At this, Alish's eyes flashed. 'You know, I think I've got just the thing.'